Cherry Cheese Pie by Carissa

SARAH LAMB

Contents

		V
1.	Chapter 1	1
2.	Chapter 2	9
3.	Chapter 3	19
4.	Chapter 4	27
5.	Chapter 5	33
6.	Chapter 6	41
7.	Chapter 7	49
8.	Chapter 8	57
9.	Chapter 9	67
10.	Chapter 10	73
11.	Chapter 11	79

12. Chapter 12 87

13. Chapter 13 93

14. Chapter 14 101

15. Chapter 15 109

16. Chapter 16 117

17. Chapter 17 121

18. Chapter 18 129

19. Chapter 19 135

20. Chapter 20 141

21. Epilogue 147

22. The True Story of the Cherry Cheese Pie 151

23. Visit everyone in Deepwater 155

24. Note from Author 160

25. About the Author 161

26. There are other great books in this series as well! 162

To my wonderful in-laws, Pat and Linda, and to the cherry cheese "courting" pie they ate that brought them together.

***

Dear Readers,
Look for that recipe at the end of this book. I promise it is not only simple, but incredibly delicious and customizable.

Chapter 1

"You are an answer to a prayer. Have I told you how glad I am that you are here?"

Carissa glanced up from the ginger cookies she was crushing for a pie crust. Her aunt Maggie, who owned the café she was working in, looked tired. Her normally frizzy hair was looked even more frazzled, and she sagged against the café's kitchen counter, one hand rubbing at the small of her back.

"It's a madhouse out there," Maggie muttered. Then she brightened. "But far be it from me to turn away business. Hank and I will be able to do a few upgrades around the place. Goodness, your pies are really packing the café."

With a laugh, Carissa shrugged and dusted off her hands. The spicy scent of ginger filled her nose. "So you say."

"So I know," her aunt corrected, wagging her finger. She picked up several small plates of pie slices that were sitting on the work table, and placed them on a tray before disappearing into the dining room.

Carissa smiled to herself as she pressed the cookie bits into the bottom of a pie pan. She was enjoying being here with her aunt. Not just in the kitchen, but also in the town. Deepwater was a quiet little place, peaceful—except for the days when the stagecoach stopped over.

Today was one of those days, and with the café the only place to eat in town, her extra hands came in handy as the passengers rushed in, hurriedly ate, and dashed out again. She wasn't sure how her aunt had managed for so long on her own running the café. Maggie's husband, Hank, helped as he could, but he also owned the livery and assisted in trading out horses for the stage stops, so he wasn't able to be there once the passengers arrived. Their young son usually helped Hank.

Carissa had only been in Deepwater for a few months, having hurried over at the bequest of her aunt following her back injury, and from the time the café opened until it closed, there was always a customer in the building. There was never a day that wasn't filled with hard work, though somehow, Carissa seemed to enjoy it as much as her aunt did.

Except for one thing.

In truth, she'd been more than eager to come when her aunt proposed the idea. Carissa was nearing thirty, and hoped the change she desired for her life would come from here. After all, it had for almost everyone else her aunt had introduced her to.

But so far, for her, it had not.

"Phew. That pie went fast." Maggie set her tray down and shook her head. "You are very talented. I count myself lucky that you came here. Your pies are something special."

Carissa flushed at her aunt's flattery. Before she could speak, though, Maggie had continued, crossing her arms over her chest. "You know what you ought to do?"

"What?" Carissa asked, beating a bowl full of cream with a little sugar. Once it had formed peaks, she'd fill the pie pan, and sprinkle more cookie crumbs on top.

"Open a bakery here." Maggie dropped a stack of dirty plates into the sink, then wiped her hands off on a towel. "You would have a line of customers out the door."

"But then who would make your pies?" Carissa asked, her eyes fixed on the cream that was starting to foam.

Maggie grew a thoughtful look. "That's true." Her face brightened. "I know! It's quite simple. You'd only sell your pies to me," she decided. "You could make other things for everyone else. Cookies. Muffins. That sort of thing."

"I see," Carissa said with a laugh.

"You'd have a popular place. I know that's something you've always wanted to do," Maggie said. "You didn't open one back home, but you could do it here. Hank and I would help you get started."

Carissa paused, and let the idea roam around in her mind for a moment. It was a generous offer. She knew Aunt Maggie and Uncle Hank would do whatever they could to help her if she asked. And, it was true she'd always longed to open a bakery. Deepwater could surely use one. But owning a business was very hard work, as she'd quickly learned by working here at the café.

There was also another problem. Carissa honestly wasn't sure if Deepwater was the town for her. The one where she wanted to settle in and open her bakery. While she promised her aunt she'd stay as long as she was needed, Carissa knew if she wanted to leave, Maggie wouldn't stop her or guilt her into staying.

"I'll think about it," was all Carissa finally said, peering into the bowl of cream. She abandoned her efforts for a moment to open the hot oven door carefully with a corner of her apron and pulled out an apple pie. Setting it onto a towel to cool, Carissa dusted the top with cinnamon.

"Be sure you do. I know you are still looking for the right path for yourself," Maggie said, slicing small wedges of cheese that would be paired with the pie once it was cooled, "but this town just has a way of bringing people in, and changing their lives. Why, I—"

"Maggie!" a voice from the dining room called.

Without hesitation, Maggie disappeared into the dining room, leaving Carissa to stare at the still-swinging door thoughtfully. It was true. She'd heard many stories of Deepwater bringing in people who hadn't intended to stay, but had.

But each of them had something she didn't. A chance at a better life. And also something that attracted another person to them. For example, Alyssa, the rejected mail-order bride, and Peter the shy postman. Theirs was an incredible story. Maggie had told it to her the first night she'd arrived, no doubt to give her hope of a future with someone special herself.

Hope was the reason she'd left for Deepwater. Just...when she arrived, the hope Carissa thought she'd packed in her carpet bag wasn't there. Why, the very reason that Carissa was eager to join her aunt and start anew was because she was tired of being a wallflower. It wasn't proper to be forward, seeking the attention of a man. Even if she had tried, it was unlikely she'd be noticed. For some reason, Carissa was someone overlooked, ignored, and unwanted by men. Someone without a single chance for anything.

Well, anything but loneliness. So far, her time in Deepwater wasn't proving to be very different from the town she'd come from.

The oldest of four, she'd smiled as each of her younger sisters had courted and then married. But each time it had happened for them, and not for her, tightness filled her chest, pain her stomach, and tears her eyes. When would it be her turn? She'd asked herself that question so many times, Carissa had lost count.

If she was being entirely honest with herself, she was starting to wonder what was wrong with her. Why wouldn't any man even look her way? Her mother had assured her it would happen. Her father had shrugged, and said men sometimes took longer than women to make up their minds. Neither of their words had helped, though she knew they were meant reassuringly.

Physically, Carissa didn't think anything was wrong with her. She was pretty enough, even if she wasn't beautiful. She smiled, laughed at jokes, was educated. Of course, she also knew her way around a kitchen. But none of that seemed to matter. Not to anyone back home, and not to anyone of the male variety here.

When her aunt's letter had come, telling of her back injury and seeing if she might be willing to spend a few months helping until she healed, Carissa was on the stage two days later. Without a beau, or even the chance at one, there was no reason not to.

A couple walked past the kitchen window, their heads nearly touching as they leaned into each other, talking and laughing about something. Carissa swallowed down the bitter jolt of jealousy, and plunged her hands into the makings of pie crust dough.

About the only thing she did well was bake. Everyone said so. So, she'd do just that, and try to forget about how empty her days—and her heart—felt.

Chapter 2

Before riding back to his ranch, Duncan Marshall decided to stop at his favorite place. Maggie's café. Just the thought of what might be served set his mouth to watering. He'd had nothing but beans and cornbread for four days straight. He was looking forward to a change.

One of these days, he was going to get himself a housekeeper to make meals so that he didn't always have to depend on the ranch hands cooking something edible or the diner when he got sick of what they burned or undercooked.

The men on his ranch, about twenty of them, took turns with meals. Duncan did occasionally as well, even though he was the boss, but by no means were any of them much good at it. A slab of meat, beans, bread, and stews tended to be the bulk of the meals for lunch or dinner. Breakfasts were usually flapjacks, oatmeal, or eggs and ham.

While that was fine for his hands, at least none of them complained, it wasn't for him. He wanted proper meals, and fully intended to find a cook for the men as well. They deserved a good meal with all the work that they did.

Duncan half wondered if he should send away for one of his sisters. He had two who were unmarried. But that might be a problem. In Deepwater, there were quite a few men who weren't wed. A good number of them on his ranch. One look at his pretty sisters who could also cook, and that would lead him right back to the problem of not having anybody to help him out. Besides, he didn't think he'd trust any of his ranch hands around his sisters.

Luckily, Maggie's café always put on a fine meal, and she was open sunrise to sundown. So, whether he was stopping in for breakfast, lunch, or dinner he could get something tasty. Which was the plan for today.

And, perhaps also part of the plan, was to see her niece. Since she'd moved into town, Duncan had been stopping in a little bit more frequently. Maggie's niece had started helping her at the café, and she was quite a baker. Her specialty was pie of all kinds. While he enjoyed each one he'd had so far, he also really enjoyed the rare glimpse he got of her.

Carissa mainly kept to the kitchen, but every now and then she'd come out. When she did, his heart started hammering like a woodpecker on a tree. He was not sure why that was because he had no intention of settling down—not with anybody and especially not with someone he hardly knew.

He told himself it was probably just the fact that he was eating a little too much pie and his brain connected his fondness of the dessert to a fondness of her. But every now and then his conscious conscience twinged annoyingly, and almost made him wonder if it was a lie.

Still, a man could look and admire someone. And he didn't plan to do more.

Slowing in front of the café, Duncan tied his horse to the post in front of the building and pushed open the door. He paused to look around.

The café was a cozy place. Of the dozen or so tables on the inside, only two were occupied. The low bar had an assortment of cups on the top, and Maggie was polishing them with a cloth. Near the back, where the large fireplace heated the room in the winter, were some comfortable chairs and an assortment of books on shelves.

Large windows let in plenty of natural light, but Maggie also had small lanterns she'd bring out and set on hooks built into the wall in the evenings.

Maggie called out a hello, and Duncan waved his hand in greeting, heading toward her.

"Here for your dinner?" Maggie asked.

"I am," he answered. "What pies do you have?"

Maggie grinned. He knew she was proud of the fact everyone was enjoying the pies her niece made. Maggie was a fine cook, and her apple pie was quite famous. Pie making must run in the family.

"We've got three today," she answered. "A rhubarb pie, a cookie pie, and a cherry cream cheese pie."

"I've never heard of that last one." Duncan asked, "What's that?"

Maggie shook her head. "I don't really know how to describe it, but I can tell you it's real tasty. I'd never had such a thing myself until a few days ago. It's a thick, creamy pie topped with sweet cooked cherries. Carissa made it up, and it's all I can do to keep it stocked today. She's made four of them, and I've sold all but one piece."

Duncan raised his brows. "Better set that one aside for me then," he said. "I want to taste it for myself and see what the fuss is all about."

With a nod, Maggie asked, "And your meal?"

A quick look at the menu Maggie had tacked to the wall was all Duncan needed. Maggie always offered two daily choices, a stew usually one of them. "I'll take the chicken and dumplings," he told her.

"It won't take me long to get it for you. Go find a seat somewhere," Maggie said, and vanished into the kitchen.

Duncan nodded and took a spot near a window. He enjoyed being able to watch people come and go as he ate his meal. Once Maggie set the bowl of chicken and dumplings down in front of him, Duncan tucked into his meal, and let his thoughts wander toward his earlier concern. Making a proper meal on his ranch a regular occurrence.

Maybe he should ask Maggie if she knew anybody who would be willing to be his housekeeper. He didn't want her thinking that she wasn't a fine cook, but at the same time it was expensive to eat too many meals out. When he was at home, he honestly didn't always enjoy eating with his ranch hands. Oh, they were a fine group of men. But the fact of the matter was sometimes he just wanted a little bit of peace and quiet. And that wasn't something he could get crowded in an outdoor kitchen with so many other men.

The café owner also knew everybody, and if there was someone seeking employment, she'd be sure to know. She'd also know the right person for the job.

Maggie appeared, seeming to sense he had finished his meal, and set down a small plate with the pie slice before him. "Tell me what you think," she urged. "Not been a person yet who hasn't loved it. The reverend and Postmaster Peter were here today for lunch and had two slices each."

"I'm glad they left me one," Duncan said. He picked up his fork and put it right into the tip of the pie. It slid down easily, meeting only a slight resistance at the crust's bottom. He raised the fork to his lips.

Right away, he could tell he never had tasted anything like this before, and it was his new favorite pie. It was fluffy and creamy. There was a slightly tart taste from the cherries, but it balanced perfectly with the sweet filling.

"This is incredible," he told Maggie. "My compliments to your niece. This might be the best pie I've ever tasted."

She nodded, a pleased expression on her face. "I thought you'd like it. Everyone does. I'll be sure to pass your words along."

Duncan took another bite. "It's no wonder she's sold out all these pies so quickly."

"Carissa is a real good baker." Maggie nodded. "I'm trying to talk her into opening a bakery here in town. Of course, people could only get her pies from me," she continued. "Now that people have gotten so used to them, I can't take that away."

Duncan laughed. "I won't lie," he said, "it's hard for me not to come here every day and see what new flavor of pie or what old favorite is on the menu."

With a wink, Maggie grinned. "That might be part of my plan."

Just then, the door to the kitchen swung open. The woman they had just been talking about stepped behind the bar and set down a pie. This one had a pie crust on top of it, and Duncan took a guess that it was the rhubarb.

"Carissa," Maggie called. "Another satisfied customer."

Carissa looked up and smiled. "I'm glad to hear so. I wouldn't know what to do with myself if someone didn't like it!"

Shaking his head, Duncan pointed to his near empty plate. "This is the best pie I have ever had. Maybe even the best thing I've ever eaten."

He didn't miss the flush that spread across her cheeks, or how Carissa ducked her head. While he had no intention of getting married, it did surprise him a little bit that she hadn't had men hanging around wanting to spend time with her. She was not only pretty, but radiated a sweetness.

"Thank you," Carissa answered softly. She drew a little bit closer to them. "Aunt Maggie, I've got two more in the oven, and I've a total of eight other pies made on the counter in the kitchen. How many pies do you want for tomorrow?"

Maggie furrowed her brow. "At the rate I'm selling, it won't hurt to have at least two more," she said. "That is, if you're not too tired to make them. I had to turn away two women who wanted to buy a whole pie each."

"Not too tired at all," Carissa said. The sweet sound of her voice made Duncan's stomach do a funny flip. He frowned, and willed it to still as he took the last bite of his pie, and she said, "I'm at your pie-making disposal. That's why I came here. To help you in the café."

She nodded once to Duncan and then turned back to the kitchen. Duncan couldn't help himself. The question came out of his mouth before he even realized that he'd asked it. "Is Carissa planning to stay in Deepwater and settle down, even after you are healed up? You mentioned her opening a bakery."

Maggie sighed. "I don't know. It would be nice, but I get the sense that no matter how much I like her being here, Deepwater hasn't turned out to give her the opportunities that she was hoping for."

"What opportunity is that?" Duncan asked. Then, he shook his head and grimaced. "Forgive me. That's a little nosy."

"Oh, not at all," Maggie said. She settled herself down comfortably in the chair across from him.

That was one thing about Maggie. She was friendly with everyone and enjoyed both hearing news and sharing it. She wasn't exactly a town gossip, for she knew when to hold her tongue, but she was well informed, one might say, and didn't mind telling what she knew.

"Well," Maggie said, her voice low. "Carissa's nearly thirty. I suspect she hoped that moving here to Deepwater would give her a fresh start on life. Help her find whatever it was she feels is missing. Possibly a husband. And that's not happened yet. I only hope it does before she decides to go back home. I'd love to have her here forever. But I'd only asked her to help for a few months, and see that I stay caught up while I recover from my back injury."

Duncan nodded. "I see." A little disappointment filled him. He wasn't really sure why. Was it the fact Carissa might leave? And why was that? He took a second to ponder that. Because of her pie making? Or because he was curious about her? Duncan wasn't sure. He couldn't fault someone for looking for what was missing in life or even someone to share their days with.

"Yes, well, that's life. Unpredictable. Nothing is decided yet," Maggie said. She pushed herself up, waving off his offer of assistance, and returned to the kitchen.

The motion of the door caught his attention, rewarding him with a glimpse of Carissa, her expression one of concentration as she measured something. Duncan stared thoughtfully at the now-closed door and wondered about his own life, and the things he felt were missing. What would life have been like had Gem not left him? Would he still feel that hollow in him?

He doubted it. He also doubted he'd be looking for a housekeeper or someone to cook for him. Gem wouldn't have done any of that, but she'd have found someone from day one, and then...and then he wouldn't have come here so often. Which meant he wouldn't have had Carissa's pies. Or glimpses of her. Or that strange tug in his chest when he thought about her.

Duncan frowned and pushed himself up. He set the money for his meal on the table and strode outside. Enough of that. He had no business having her on his mind so much. After all, he'd hardly said more than a handful of words to Carissa since she'd arrived in Deepwater. To top it off, he was not interested in any sort of a relationship with anyone. So, why would her comings or goings affect him?

They wouldn't.

He ignored the nudges in his mind, and instead mounted his horse and rode back to his ranch. The housekeeper problem could wait a while longer. He passed a few people and waved. The action lightened the ache in his chest a little. Deepwater was a friendly little town. And that's all he was. Friendly to everyone he met. His attention and thoughts to Maggie's niece Carissa would be nothing more than the same.

Chapter 3

Carissa peered through the café's kitchen window, watching as Duncan went into the post office. He'd come to the café several times a week since she'd been there. More, Maggie said, than she'd seen him ever do.

Perhaps it was the pies. Goodness knew they flew out of the pie tins almost as fast as she got them in there. Maggie had ordered another dozen from the general store. But she was still curious about him. Didn't he have a cook himself? She knew he wasn't married. There were a lot of unmarried men in town—not that any had even so much as looked at her—but she also knew he had a ranch, and likely employed ranch hands. So, who cooked for them? The person must not be very good since he was coming here so frequently.

As she pondered the question, the post office door reopened, and Duncan came out, a letter in hand. Carissa stepped back from the window suddenly. What on earth was she doing spying on the man? She'd never stared at anyone before, so why him? And why now?

Simply curious about the town and its people, she decided, that's all she was. Then she bit her lip and wondered if that was a lie. She didn't make a habit of watching what anyone else did. What was it about him that made her follow his every move?

"Carissa?"

She turned, and her aunt stood at the kitchen door. "Yes?"

"I've got to run a bite down to Hank. He's helping the reverend at the church. I'll likely be gone a half hour. Will you watch the café for me?"

"Of course," Carissa said, and came out into the main area.

It was quiet right now, and likely would be so for a while. The lunch rush had passed, so all she had to do was sit for a little with a cup of tea and relax. Something she could easily do. It was hot in the kitchen, and she'd been making pies all morning. A break was more than welcome.

She heard the sound of the kitchen's door leading outside open, then close, and spotted Maggie with a basket in hand heading toward the church. Carissa yawned, and sipped at her tea. The only downside to working at the café was how early they had to get up, long before the sun did, in order to start cooking for the day.

Though, if she opened a bakery, it would likely be the same. And she'd be responsible for doing everything herself. Carissa still wasn't sure what she thought about that idea. She enjoyed making baked goods for others to enjoy, but just as it was really too much work for her aunt to run the café on her own, she had the feeling it would be the same if she were to open a bakery.

The small bell over the café's door jingled, and Carissa smiled as Laura, the reverend's wife, walked in. Laura was about her age, and had made Carissa feel welcome the moment she'd moved here.

"Hello!" Carissa greeted her.

"Hello," Laura answered, and then sniffed the air. "What's in the oven? Peach pies?"

Carissa laughed. "Yes. How did you guess?"

Laura grinned. "My grandmother used to make peach pies. I loved them dearly. It's been a while since I've had one. Are they for today or tomorrow?"

"Tomorrow," Carissa told her. "Today is cherry pie, sugar cream pie, or blackberry pie."

"Mmm! I'd like a slice of the blackberry," Laura said. "And some tea. I'll be back tomorrow for peach."

"Sure, give me just a moment," Carissa said.

She went into the kitchen and a moment later had the requested items on a tray. Laura was sitting at a table near the window that faced the stream.

"Here you are," Carissa said.

"Can you join me for a few moments?" Laura asked.

"I can. Let me get my tea," Carissa said. She returned to the kitchen and got herself a slice of the blackberry pie as well.

When she slipped into a chair at the table, Laura smiled at her over her teacup. "Well, it's been a few weeks since I last asked. Enjoying Deepwater still? Have you met most everyone?"

"I might have," Carissa said, "though I'm sure there are some I've not crossed paths with yet. I don't have too much time to socialize. Aunt Maggie keeps me busy."

"You are an absolute blessing to her," Laura said. "When she hurt her back, I knew she was terrified about the running of the café. I offered several times, but I'm not sure she trusted me in her kitchen."

"I'm happy to be here," Carissa admitted. "It is good to have a change of scenery."

"Even if it's just trading one kitchen for another?" Laura teased.

Carissa thought about that for a moment. The reverend's wife might have been making a joke, but it brought something to mind. The fact that though her aunt wouldn't mind a bit if she did leave the kitchen more, Carissa really hadn't. Why was that?

"Hmm," she said. "You know, back home, I really didn't spend as much time in the kitchen as I do now. Of course, I'm helping Aunt Maggie, but..."

"But?" Laura prompted.

"Well, I guess I like the kitchen here. It feels...secure."

"In what way?" Laura asked. "Has something here unsettled you?" Her face looked concerned.

"Not for my safety," Carissa hurried to assure her. She picked up her tea, then said, "It's just while everyone's nice, I am struggling a little to feel like I fit in somewhere. I thought in coming here, I'd help my aunt and just sort of find what I was looking for in my life. That hasn't happened yet. The second part, I mean."

Laura nodded as she finished a bite of pie. "Deepwater has attracted several people who are trying to find the right paths for themselves."

"That's what Aunt Maggie says," Carissa said, feeling frustrated. "Yet, it seems they've found them, and I have not."

"It will happen," Laura assured her. She nodded toward the post office. "Alyssa had a difficult time when she first arrived. Her first moments here in Deepwater were very unwelcome, when she was rejected on the spot by the man she'd come to marry."

Carissa looked surprised. "That part I didn't know," she said.

"It's quite a story. Myself," Laura grinned, "I didn't even want to be here when my stagecoach broke. Your aunt, however, made me feel right at home, and I grew to love Deepwater."

"Saved it, too. And her life," Carissa said. She smiled. "Aunt Maggie loves to tell your story. I think she's done that once a week since I came."

Laura laughed and shook her head. "My point is, there are other stories about the people in this town, and who knows? Maybe one will someday be yours."

"Maybe," Carissa said doubtfully. "But speaking of stories, do you know Duncan Marshall? What can you tell me about him?"

Nodding, Laura said, "I do. He lives not too far from here. Owns a good-sized ranch. A mix of livestock, from what I understand."

"He's come in pretty often, yet I know nothing about him," Carissa mused. "He doesn't talk too much."

"That sounds about right," Laura said. "He's quiet, and always keeps to himself." She leaned close and whispered, even though it was just the two of them, "I sense a story about that."

"What kind of a story?" Carissa whispered in reply.

Laura shook her head, then sipped on her tea. As she put the cup down, she shrugged. "I couldn't speculate. I only know that more than one woman has tried to catch his eye, and he's not gone for any of them."

"I wish I had that problem," Carissa sighed. "A line of men waiting for me, I mean. I don't even have one."

"It will happen if it's meant to," Laura said. She reached over and squeezed Carissa's hand. "Do not ever think that if you don't have a man, there is something wrong with you. There isn't. It is better to wait for the right one to come along than to rush into something and have a bad experience."

"But what if he never comes?" Carissa asked.

Laura laughed. "Have you ever known a man to be on time?"

She couldn't help it. Carissa's lips twitched, and soon she was laughing with Laura. Though her heart felt much lighter, and she knew the reverend's wife was right, she still wished—desperately—that one day, the right man would come along.

The café door opened, and a few ranch hands walked in, talking loudly. Carissa stood and smiled, walking over to them. Who knows? Maybe she just needed to look harder.

Chapter 4

Duncan eased open the door to the café and looked around. Though he'd tried not to come as often, the lure of the pies, and Carissa, were too great of a temptation.

After church one Sunday, Maggie had invited him to join their picnic—invite being the polite word. Forced would be more accurate.

However, after the initial awkwardness faded, he found himself enjoying Maggie and Hank's company, and Carissa's as well. She was not only beautiful, she was smart too. Her knowledge extended beyond baking, and over cold fried chicken and buttermilk biscuits, he discovered she had an inquisitive mind as she asked questions about his ranch.

"Goodness, you manage all of that on your own?" Carissa had asked that first Sunday, her eyes wide as he told her how many heads of cattle he had.

"I've got hands to help run the ranch," he said as his cheeks heated, though he wasn't sure why. "They do a lot. Couldn't run the place without them."

"Some have stopped in the café, I think," Carissa told him.

"Everyone does, for your pie," Maggie had interjected proudly.

"That's because we need something tasty now and again," Duncan had laughed. "You don't want to try my cooking."

Carissa had continued asking about his ranch each time they shared a Sunday lunch, and he was only too happy to answer her, and her follow-up questions. Duncan found himself looking forward to Sunday afternoons, and their conversations. Sometimes, they'd go for a short walk on the path by the church, and other times they'd just sit. He wasn't sure when it had happened, but he'd started thinking of her as a friend.

She seemed genuinely interested in him and what he did. It was different. Felt nice. There was no pressure. No expectation. A far cry from how Gem had been.

Gem. She'd been haunting his memories as of late. Was it because he and Carissa had formed a friendship? Would that woman always try and ruin his life? She'd already done it once. Wasn't that good enough?

He gave a bitter laugh. Not likely. Gem would make sure he was miserable for the rest of his days.

"What's that frown for?" Carissa asked.

Duncan froze, shook himself from his thoughts, and then grinned. "Just worried all the pies will be gone," he said, hiding the truth. No one in town knew what had really happened with Gem, except for Reverend Gabriel Sullivan, but they were friends, and Gabriel would never tell anyone.

"For my best customer? You get your pick," Maggie said from where she was wiping a table. "Strawberry, pumpkin, or a cherry cheese pie."

"Cherry cheese," Duncan said, without hesitation. "Though they are all good, there's just something about that one."

"I heard tell Clyde and Linda started courting right after they shared a slice," Maggie said. "That pie has a way of bringing people together."

Duncan didn't miss the sly look she was giving him. It seemed like Carissa didn't either. She rolled her eyes at her aunt, and she held out the plate. "Thanks," he said, taking the slice from her. Their fingers brushed, and he felt a tiny zap. That happened though, sometimes when it was cool or dry out. That was all, he told himself.

"Phew, it's hot out," Maggie said, a hand massaging her lower back, "and so humid. Wonder when we will get a little cooler and drier weather."

"Why don't you rest for a time, Aunt Maggie?" Carissa asked, her brows knitting together. "You've been on your feet too long."

Maggie hesitated, but then nodded. "Perhaps just a little. My back is hurting. I'll be in the kitchen with my feet up." She left, and Carissa brought a cup of tea over and sat with Duncan.

He tried not to feel pleased, and instead focus on polite conversation, but it was hard.

Carissa couldn't sit for long, though. Soon, customers flooded the café, and she and Maggie were busily serving them. He couldn't help but scowl as three of his hands walked in, fixing Carissa with their best smiles and being polite as she served them. He tried not to let it upset him.

He also wondered why it bothered him.

Laughter came from the table, and he saw Carissa joining in, her cheeks flushed and her eyes sparkling. Had one of his men been flirting with her? Or just telling jokes? As curious as he was, Duncan didn't want to stick around. A wave of something akin to jealousy washed over him, and he quickly stood, dropped his money on the table, and set out toward his ranch.

When he arrived, he left his boots on the porch and walked inside. His home was a stark contrast to the café.

He used to enjoy the quiet, even if it felt a little too loud at times. Now, he didn't really enjoy it. It felt too empty.

Duncan roamed the house, not quite sure what to do with himself. Oh, there was always work, to be sure, but he felt restless, and wasn't quite understanding why. Was something amiss in the house?

He checked the kitchen, with its large stove and sturdy wooden table, then walked past the living room, three bedrooms, a room he used for an office, and settled himself into the large chair he had before a desk. Everything seemed fine, so what was bothering him?

Could it still be the image of Carissa smiling, her hand on one of the men's shoulders as they all laughed together? He held his breath, then let it out. It was time to stop thinking about her.

Duncan tried to look over his mail he'd collected, but that restless feeling persisted. It was too quiet. Too empty. Was that why he enjoyed the café? The bustling of the place, the noise of the diners? Well, his hands excluded.

But that couldn't be it. He'd learned the times that were the quietest at the café, so he could stop in, enjoy a bite, and have a little conversation with Carissa.

Carissa. Also a woman who wouldn't stop racing through his mind. Though she was different from Gem, and they were only friends, Duncan still felt hesitant around her at times. And he wasn't sure why.

They enjoyed each other's company. That much was fact. Carissa also didn't pressure him. Didn't ask for more. In the weeks he'd known her, he'd grown grateful for her. She didn't press him for his secrets, didn't make suggestions or hints about a future with him.

But that almost made him wonder why. Until he thought about Gem again, and he knew why. He wasn't good enough. She'd made that clear. Before their wedding day, she'd told him over and over how he needed to do more, try harder, and she'd finally gotten so disgusted, she didn't even bother to show up for their wedding.

Duncan blew out a deep breath and looked around the study. His room. The way he liked it. A large fireplace for the winter. Books on a shelf. A haphazard stack of papers on his desk. The remnants of a meal sitting on a side table. This was him. The real him. A man who worked hard, wasn't perfect, was messy, but who gave his all no matter what he did in life.

And that was exactly why he was never, ever, going to get involved with another woman again. It was his nature to give all he had, but another experience with heartache was something he just couldn't risk. So, when it came to Carissa, he continued to offer friendship, and nothing more.

Chapter 5

"What do you think?" The shoemaker gestured to the empty building, then put his hands on his hips as he admired it. "I spent many a happy year in here. I'm grateful for my new building, but I'm also excited to hear you are considering opening a bakery—possibly in here."

"Nothing is set yet," Carissa said hurriedly. "I am just looking, at Aunt Maggie's request."

"Don't feel pressured," the shoemaker said. "Not by me, nor your aunt. She means well, but never you mind if this won't work for you. I'll find someone to rent it to. Quickly, as well, I bet. If it's not right for you, don't say yes. You take your time and look around for a few minutes. Come get me if you have any questions. I'll be in my shop."

Carissa nodded, and wandered through the building. Her footsteps, though light, still echoed in the empty rooms as she examined each. There was a storefront and a large backroom, both with several windows. The backroom would make for a fair-sized kitchen. Perhaps not as large as she'd like. Would it be big enough? In truth, she wasn't sure, once worktables and a large oven were installed.

Carissa tried to imagine how much room there would be. One person could manage, but could two or three? It might be a tight fit. Still, if the rest of the place suited, then she might consider it.

In the corner of the room, a flight of stairs led to two small rooms upstairs. Living quarters, the shoemaker had told her.

Carissa glanced from the windows and spotted Maggie inside the café chatting with someone. A little bit of guilt filled her. She knew her aunt wanted her to stay. Was even encouraging her to open a bakery. Just...something about the idea didn't feel right. Knowing what to do felt difficult.

On the one hand, she really did need to make money and set it by for her old age. Without a husband, she'd need to care for herself and all of her life expenses. Her talents didn't lie in dressmaking or some other sort of trade. No, her skill was in the kitchen. Primarily baking.

That led to the option of working for a restaurant or owning an eatery herself. Since she had no interest in being competition for her aunt, a bakery was a natural solution. She'd hopefully be able to find someone to help run the front counter while she made all of her pies and sweet rolls in the kitchen.

But that sounded lonely. Sounded like she might eventually get tired of doing that. Of working by herself all of the time. That's why she enjoyed the café and her aunt's constant chatter.

It was also difficult and hard work. Uncle Hank always hoisted the large bags of flour and sugar. If she were in the kitchen on her own, how would she manage? Not to mention that was a great deal of baking for just one person. Right now, she was simply making pies and bread. Add in cookies, cakes, pastries...how could she manage that entirely on her own, even if someone did help at the counter?

Carissa walked down the stairs and studied the possible kitchen once more before walking outside. She gave the two rooms a long, considering look. Going outside, she closed the building door and walked to the shoemaker's shop. He glanced up from his bench where he was working on a boot and set down his tools.

"What do you think?" he asked her, crossing his arms over his chest.

"It's a wonderful location, and I love the rooms above, but I'm afraid it might be too small of a kitchen area," Carissa told him honestly.

She decided not to mention any other reason for her hesitation, especially the reluctance she was feeling at the idea of starting a bakery.

"I think you might be right," the shoemaker told her. "Don't you feel bad," he continued. "I'm sure you'll find the perfect place if you do open one. Even if Hank has to build it for you."

"There's an idea," Carissa agreed.

She said goodbye, and as she stepped through the door and onto the street, she walked right into someone. "Oh! I'm so sorry," she gasped, trying to steady herself without grabbing onto them. Though she had stumbled, whoever she'd collided into was a very solid individual, and didn't budge an inch.

Two strong hands firmly took her elbows, and when Carissa's embarrassed face glanced up, she was surprised to see Duncan looking down at her.

"Hello," he said with a grin. "Fancy running into you."

The joke was so ridiculous, Carissa laughed. He joined in, and Carissa couldn't help but feel grateful it was him she'd run into, not someone else.

"I'm sorry, I wasn't watching where I was going," she told him.

"No harm done," he told her.

His hands stayed where they were, and Carissa's heart started to flutter. She glanced at his face. There were tiny crinkles in the corners of his eyes. She'd never noticed those before, but she liked them. At that moment, he seemed to notice he was still holding her. He quickly dropped his hands and took a half step backward. Carissa felt disappointment seeping through her, but she tried to ignore it.

"So," Duncan said, nodding toward the door she'd just come out of. "Getting new shoes?"

"No," Carissa said. "I was looking at his old shop for a potential bakery site."

Duncan raised his brows. "You think you might open one?"

"I'm really not sure," Carissa said. "This building wasn't right for me. Truthfully...I know Aunt Maggie wants me to open one, and I enjoy what I do, but the idea of opening a bakery...It's not something that one person could do alone. As much as I'd likely enjoy it at times, I don't know if it's the right thing for me."

"Any idea what is?" Duncan asked.

They started to slowly walk down the street, falling into sync as though they'd done this every day of their lives.

It was a good question, and one she'd asked herself many times. But, no matter how many she had, or the fact others had asked it of her, the answer was always the same. Somehow, though, with Duncan she didn't feel the need to make an excuse or give him some vague answer.

"I enjoy making pies for the café," Carissa said. "But as for what's the right thing for me, I just don't know," she admitted. "I'm trying so hard to figure it out. This is my fourth month here. I felt so sure, based on Aunt Maggie's stories, that once I arrived, I'd have everything figured out."

"I'm not sure anyone, anywhere, really has everything figured out," Duncan told her. He scratched at his chin. "I can tell you, for one, I sure don't."

"No?" Carissa glanced at him. "But you are on your way, it seems. Your ranch is successful."

"I work hard," he agreed, "because I have a lot of men depending on me to provide for them and their families. It's a little scary at times."

"I bet it is," Carissa said, and shuddered. "Here, I'm wondering just how to take care of myself in my older years. You have to think about not only yourself, but all those others."

Duncan shrugged so slightly she almost missed it. "It's a privilege," he told her. "And something that I try not to take lightly. Each time I expand a little further, I thank God for His help."

They were in front of the café now, but Carissa didn't want to go inside. She didn't want their conversation to end. Though over the last few months she'd gotten to know Duncan better, especially as he was now a regular at their Sunday afternoon picnics, this conversation felt different. More serious. Intimate. As though what he was telling her wasn't something that he'd tell most people.

"Do you...do you have to leave to head home? Or do you have time for a slice of pie and a cup of coffee?"

"I'd like that," he agreed, and opened the café door, holding it for her.

Carissa's breath sucked in quickly as she walked inside. Had that been his hand brushing against her lower back? She certainly tingled there.

She went into the kitchen and returned a moment later with two slices of oatmeal pie, his coffee, and a tea for her. While the conversation took a different turn as Maggie joined them, Carissa didn't mind. The familiar ache had settled in her chest, reminding her that her path had never been clear. Not in anything that was related to her future.

It was frustrating and disappointing, both at once. Not just that she didn't know what to do about having a bakery, but also that no matter how much she'd wanted to hope for something more than friendship with a man, it had never happened.

Here, it had been the same. In all truthfulness, Carissa didn't want just any man. She wanted Duncan. Though a few other men in town had flattered her, she knew that was all it was. They weren't serious. It was Duncan, though, who had caught her eye.

Too often, she found herself watching him as he walked past. Thinking about him in quiet moments. Staring at him on Sundays or when he came into the café.

It was all one-sided, of course. It didn't seem he was interested in anything more than being friends.

Was friendship enough, though? Carissa wasn't sure. It was better than nothing. And nothing was what she'd had most of her life. Perhaps that would be all she had in her future.

Carissa studied Duncan from under her eyelashes for a moment before she decided. Yes, a friendship with Duncan was better than nothing. She could be content with that. Though she wanted much more, she'd rather have him in her life than not.

Chapter 6

Duncan drew in a deep breath and let it out slowly as he rode across the pasture, counting the heads of his newest cattle. Seeing Carissa today had been nice. What wasn't, was she'd decided against renting the space for her bakery, and the fact she wasn't even sure if she wanted to open one.

He was being selfish, he knew. But if she had a bakery, she'd have a reason to stay in Deepwater. That would give him more time to consider what he'd like to do one day. Oh, he knew what he wanted to do—and that was tell her he liked her. But he also wasn't ready to get caught up in another relationship ever again.

What he also wanted was a deep friendship that grew into something more. Perhaps over a few years. Slowly, naturally, things could progress. But he might not get that.

A touch of worry filled his gut as he remembered her face. There was a hint of sadness in her eyes, though she'd tried to hide it. When she spoke, there was a little catch in her words. She sounded like she was a little unhappy here. Like something was keeping her from fully embracing Deepwater.

Or was it someone? Was one of his hands—who he knew had been hanging around the café—bothering her and she didn't like it? He tensed at the idea. He'd been considering telling them to stay away from her, but then that would mean they'd assume—even if rightfully so—that he was interested in Carissa.

The problem was, it wouldn't be fair to her to be kept waiting for him to decide if he wanted to pursue a relationship or not. It felt like Duncan was in an endless spiral of both longing to tell Carissa how he felt, then wanting to wait and see what happened.

There were problems with both events, and he just wasn't sure which one was the right course of action. Or if neither was. Maybe he shouldn't even let himself think about falling in love.

But it might be too late. His heart certainly thought so.

"All of 'em here?" Pete, his foreman asked, riding up.

"Looks it. Good stock," Duncan said, glad to be pulled from his thoughts. "You chose them well."

"Thank you." Pete rubbed at his forehead and tipped his hat up. "Enjoy your pie earlier?"

Duncan pretended he didn't see the other man's smirk. "It's nice Maggie always has a few to choose from," he said instead.

"That's what Claude, Mark, and Kyle say," Pete said. "You better lay your claim down. They are placing bets between themselves who Carissa'll end up with. All three of them are interested in her."

Duncan tensed. What should he say? There he was, back in that spiral he'd just been pulled from. His mind spun, and so did his stomach. If he shrugged and acted like it wasn't a problem, then he might not get to have a chance with Carissa. If he admitted he liked her, word might get around. And him being the source of gossip was something he didn't want.

"That so?" Duncan finally said. "If they'd pay half as much attention to their work as they did the local women..."

There. That was a safe reply.

"Uh huh. Why don't you just admit it? You like Maggie's niece," Pete said. "I'm warning you. You best let them, and her, know. Don't do any good to make a woman in a town full of unmarried men wait."

"I—"

Pete was spared from what Duncan was about to say when another ranch hand rode up. He was shouting something they strained to hear, but it was obvious something was wrong. He drew closer, and they made out the words.

"Fire at the schoolhouse!" the man shouted, then wheeled his horse around, heading toward town.

With a quick glance at each other, Duncan and Pete followed, spurring the horses to go as fast as they could.

Fire was dangerous. There hadn't been rain for a while, which made it even more worrying. With buildings so close to one another, if the wind picked up and it spread before it was contained, things could be very bad.

The fact it was at the school made him even more worried. Duncan prayed that no one was hurt.

The men pushed their horses and made good time. When they arrived, a crowd was gathered around the school building. Duncan couldn't see flames, but there was plenty of smoke in the air. He pushed his way through the townsfolk until he saw Gabriel. "What happened?" he asked.

"One of the students stacked the books too close to the stove before they went out to play at lunch. Best we can figure is while Laura was heating a kettle of water, and went outside to eat her lunch, a spark blew out of the stove somehow, landed on a book, and caught fire." Gabriel shook his head. "The building is okay. A little scorching. But all of the schoolbooks are a total loss."

"That's terrible," Duncan said.

"Laura feels awful," Gabriel sighed. "Even though it's not her fault. I think we'll need to do some sort of fundraising to get new books. The children must have them, but the financial burden is too great for any one person to bear."

"I'll help however I can," Duncan promised, relieved to see the building was still standing, and no one was hurt. Their town didn't have a proper doctor, and a major injury would be a problem.

Gabriel clapped him on the arm and turned as a parent came up to him. Duncan stepped back, intending to return to his horse, as he wasn't needed. Thankfully. Things could have turned out far worse than they had. He knew the entire town was going to be grateful for that. Parents, especially.

Someone bumped into him right then, and just as they apologized, he grinned. "We've got to stop meeting like this."

Carissa looked up at him, her eyes nearly sparkling as she laughed. "You must think me the clumsiest person around," she told him.

"If clumsy is another word for incredible pie maker and good friend, then yes. I do," Duncan teased.

She smiled up at him, and it took every ounce of Duncan not to brush off the smudge of flour across her nose and cheek. He forced himself to repeat the words he'd just said. Good friend. Nothing more.

"It's a terrible thing," she said then, her face clouding over as she looked toward the school.

"Yes, but I'm sure glad the building is standing, and no one is hurt," Duncan said. "It will take some effort to replace the books, but we will."

Carissa nodded. "Yes. I am sure. I have heard stories of the people in this town pulling together on more than one occasion. I'm sad about the circumstance, but glad to be a part of pulling together this time."

Silence filled the air. It wasn't uncomfortable, but Duncan knew he ought to say something.

Reluctantly, Carissa took a half step back. "I guess I best get back to the café. Aunt Maggie sent me to help when we heard the shouts of fire. No doubt she's worried. She will be relieved to hear all is well."

Duncan nodded, and raised his hand in farewell. He watched as Carissa walked back toward the café.

Gabriel appeared at his elbow. "I wonder," he mused.

"Wonder what?" Duncan asked.

"I wonder if the two of you realize that you like the other," the reverend said.

Duncan opened his mouth and started to sputter an answer, but Gabriel wasn't there any longer. He might have thought he'd imagined the words, but for the fact he saw the reverend strolling away, hands jammed into his pockets and a whistle on his lips.

Growling, Duncan mounted to his horse and headed back home. What was with everyone today? First Pete, now Gabriel? Even if he might like Carissa, he had his plan. If he chose it. Slow and steady. A long friendship. Perhaps something more one day. Many, many days away.

He wasn't in a rush. The problem, though, was he wasn't sure if she was. And now, his foreman was telling him a few of his men were interested in her. That complicated things. Especially if she liked one of them.

A little unease filled his gut, but Duncan tried to ignore it. Carissa was easy to be around. That's likely why the men liked her. Maybe for no other reason. He knew he felt relaxed when he was with her. Probably too relaxed. Here, he'd almost told her his story earlier when they'd been walking together.

Walking together. What might that be like? Just strolling along, no place to go, nowhere to be? Just the two of them. Together. Talking about whatever happened to come to mind.

Duncan straightened in his saddle, and his scowl wiped the silly grin off his face that he had been wearing. Something was wrong with him. Must be some sort of fever from the heat. He knew better than to think this way.

And he wouldn't do it again.

Chapter 7

Carissa looked up as the café door opened. The reverend strode in and walked over to her as she stood behind the counter. "Hello," he greeted, with his usual cheerful smile.

"How are you?" Carissa asked.

She always enjoyed her interactions with Gabriel. He was most unlike any reverend she'd ever known. Part of that was his unusual background, and what had made him become a reverend. It gave him perspectives that many others might not have.

"I am feeling better now that I have a plan to help replace the school's books," he told her.

"A plan, huh?" Maggie asked, coming out from the kitchen and wiping her hands on her apron. "I thought that was Laura's area."

Gabriel laughed, and his eyes filled with humor. "I'm learning from the best," he joked.

"What's your idea?" Carissa asked. "If there is a way we can help, we will."

"That's why I've come," he told her. "I am visiting every family in town. I'd like to have a pie auction."

"A pie auction?" Maggie asked.

Carissa shook her head. "I'm not sure what that is."

"I'm asking anyone who is willing to do it, to make a pie. Next Saturday, it's a holiday here anyway. We are celebrating the founding of Deepwater. As planned, we'll get together for a potluck dinner, but afterward auction off the pies."

"And you think people will buy them?" Carissa asked. "I mean, I'm sure people will buy them," she corrected herself. "What I meant was, will you make enough to replace the books?"

Gabriel nodded, and winked. "We will if Maggie makes her apple pie and you make your cherry cheese pie."

"I'll make it for sure," Maggie said.

"Just one each," Gabriel said, holding up a finger. "That's part of the plan. The bidding will be higher if people realize there's just the one."

"Good idea," Maggie agreed.

"I'll be happy to contribute," Carissa said. "If you need anything else, please be sure to let me know."

"I will," Gabriel promised, and then turned, waving a hand in farewell as he pushed open the door.

"What a fine idea," Maggie said. "There are a few men who get a little competitive. I bet the pies bring in enough for those books. And, of course, whatever woman bakes the pie that makes the most money, well, they get some bragging rights too!"

Carissa laughed at her aunt's expression of bright eyes and a wide grin as she rubbed her hands together. "Is that so?" she asked.

"Oh yes," Maggie said. She leaned in and whispered, "I've been looking for a chance to show a person or two that my pies are better."

"Aunt Maggie!" Carissa gasped. "I'd have never thought that about you."

"And I'll deny it until the end." Her aunt winked. Then, she smiled a sly grin. "What if it's a handsome gentleman who wins yours, and he asks you to enjoy it with him?"

It was all Carissa could do not to snort at the ridiculous idea. "That won't happen," she scoffed.

"It might," her aunt said.

"That's unlikely," Carissa said. She picked up a kitchen rag and wiped it across the bar, using the hurt that fueled her to scrub at an invisible mark.

"What about those ranch hands?" her aunt asked. "They've been hanging around a good deal. You like one of those?"

Rolling her eyes and refusing to look at her aunt, Carissa said, "I'm not interested in them, and they are just flirting with me because there aren't many women in town. One's already got a sweetheart, and the other two don't plan to settle. I can tell. I've the feeling that I'm a little more than a bet."

"That can't be true," her aunt said. Then she narrowed her eyes. "Though, I wouldn't put it past them. I know that Kyle is one of those very competitive men."

"Which explains the sly winks and the dollars I've seen changing hands," Carissa sighed. She shook her head. "It doesn't hurt my feelings they act like that, because I'm not interested in them. Who I do like doesn't seem the least bit interested in me. And therein lies the problem! Aunt Maggie, I think it's time that I simply realize no man I want to get to know better is going to be interested in me in the way I hope for," Carissa said, fighting the stinging in her eyes.

"I'm okay with that, I am," she continued, slowing her frantic scrubbing as the hurt and anger fled, leaving her only with sadness.

"I don't need someone to make me happy. I'm generally very content with my life. It's just...I would like someone to love. And someone to love me. But I won't settle. I won't just take someone because it's an offer of pity or desperation sinks in."

"And you shouldn't," Maggie said firmly. "But I won't lie. When I see there's a man very obviously in love with you, and he won't tell you, it makes me right mad. I'm about to give him a piece of my mind."

"Oh no," Carissa said, and put her hands on her hips. "Don't you dare embarrass me that way. I'm sure you're wrong, and then we'll have someone scared to come into the café. How will that look? And if you mean Duncan, it simply isn't true."

Her aunt's chin jutted out. "I know you think me a busybody. It's true, I am. But with good reason. I see things others don't. And right now, I know there's a gentleman interested in you, just he's too scared to say anything. But why he's dragging his feet, I'll never know."

She opened her mouth to say something more when they heard Hank calling from the kitchen. Maggie turned without another word, and Carissa huffed out a deep breath.

"If someone's interested in me," she muttered, "he'd better stop dragging his feet before I walk out of here on my own."

Her aunt's idea was preposterous. There wasn't anyone wanting more than a friendship with her. If there was, surely she'd have noticed. There'd have been signs. Like when each of her sisters had callers. The man would stop by often, linger. Laugh and smile. Make conversation.

The ranch hands didn't count. They were customers. They came in and hurried out. There was no lingering. No silent moments filled with words that were unspoken, or a kind of tension filling the air.

Why, the only one who did linger was Duncan. A time or two she'd thought he was holding back something he wanted to say, but he'd never said it, not in all the weeks or months she'd been here. She had given up hope on him. It was easier that way. There was no hurt if she rejected him, instead of it being the other way around.

Carissa glanced through the window. Now that Duncan was on her mind, she wondered when she'd see him next. He hadn't come in today. He didn't come in every day, but he did come quite often, and it had been two days since he'd been there, and she was curious where he was.

When she made her pie, would he bid on it? Ask her to join him in a slice? She didn't want anyone else to win it. Even if they didn't share it, just knowing he had cared enough to bid on it...outspend any other man so that just he could have it. Would he? Would that gesture show he cared for her? Or would he do it just out of friendship?

Carissa let herself think about that for a moment. Wonder about it. A smile formed as she thought about him. Duncan always did that to her. She remembered how, twice now, she'd bumped into him. How he'd steadied her each time. Hadn't embarrassed her.

They'd been so close, and she hadn't felt nervous at all. Hadn't felt anything but comfortable, and content to be next to him. Close to him.

Carissa drew in a deep breath, then released it slowly. "If it was love, I'd have felt tingles. Not comfortable. That was his feeling of friendship. Not more."

She was right, wasn't she? Carissa was sure of it. It didn't matter that her mind kept going back to that moment, and each of the other times that they'd been close.

Picking up an abandoned cup, Carissa returned to the kitchen. There were pies to make, not daydreams of romance to be had.

Chapter 8

"Anything else you want me to take to the post office?" Duncan asked as he swung onto the wagon and took up the reins.

"I think Beck is coming with his letter to that girl he likes," Pete said. He squinted and raised a hand to shield his eyes from the sun. "Yep. Here he is."

The young man in question ran up, and offered the envelope. "Thanks, Mr. Marshall," he said.

"No problem." Duncan stowed the letter with the others in his wagon. With nothing else, he released the wagon's brake, and headed into town to pick up supplies from the general store and visit the post office.

If there was time, he'd like to stop in and see Carissa. For a slice of pie. That was it. Nothing more. Well, maybe just to say hello. After all, they were friends. But that was it. Friends only. For a good while yet.

Duncan nodded to himself, sure in his plan. Slow and steady was what won the race. The race in question being the one toward a marriage. After being betrayed by Gem, there was no hurry. None at all. It was obvious to him that Carissa felt the same, as she wasn't making it known to anyone in town that she'd like a relationship.

He'd overheard his men talking. They were interested in her all right, but she'd not shown signs of wanting them.

Fine by him. Maybe she was of the same mind of taking things slow. In fact, a lifelong friendship would work well too. No expectations. No hurt, then, either. Even if Duncan thought he might be falling in love with Carissa, he'd be just as happy admiring her from a distance, letting his daydreams wander. It was safer that way.

Though years had passed since Gem broke his heart, he hadn't quite healed. Or...maybe it was that he had, but he was more careful now. Not in a rush to experience such pain again, if something were to not work out.

There he went again, Duncan sighed to himself. Moving into those swirling thoughts that led to him feeling even more confused than ever. It was like when a piece of string was tied in a circle, and you go around and around looking for the start and can't seem to find it.

It was best not to think about it at all. Not to think about Gem, not to think about Carissa, not to think about love or relationships.

Just not think.

The ride to town didn't take too long, and soon he was swinging off the wagon seat and walking up to the post office window.

"Well, hello!" Alyssa, Peter's wife, smiled brightly at him. "You've got a few letters," she said.

"I've also got a few from the men, for the next outgoing mail," Duncan said, setting them down on the window ledge.

"I'll be sure they go out," Alyssa promised, and she handed him over a bundle. "Here you are."

"Say, I've not been to town for a few days," he said. "Have you heard anything about the fundraiser to buy schoolbooks for the children? I know Gabriel was wanting to do something. If I can help, I will."

"I have," Alyssa answered. "You'll enjoy this one, I'm sure. The town is buzzing about it. Saturday there's going to be a big potluck picnic. For the meal only. All the desserts have to be bid on. There's going to be a pie auction, and every woman in town was asked to make one pie for it. Gabriel and Peter went to every home."

"I see. I suspect there will be a good turnout," Duncan said as he started to flip through the mail Alyssa had given him.

"Are you planning to bid on any of the pies?" Alyssa asked. Then she teased, "I know how much you love pie, especially those ones that Carissa makes."

Duncan glowered at her. "What is it with everyone in this town giving me a hard time about going over to the café and having a slice of pie now and again?" he asked.

"Not a thing," Alyssa answered, "except for the fact that you are completely oblivious to the fact that you like Carissa and she likes you."

Duncan stiffened. Only half of that was right, and he wasn't about to admit it. He was fully aware that he liked Carissa, but that wasn't any of Alyssa's business.

"Well, none of that matters," Duncan said, "true or not. Not when I'm not planning to do anything about it."

He fixed her with a look, but Alyssa just laughed. The sound irritated him, even though he knew she wasn't trying to be unkind.

"Anything else I can do for you?" she asked as another customer approached.

"That's it. Thank you."

He walked away from the window and paused. Did he want to go to the café now? He was sure that Alyssa was standing there watching him. Even as she helped Mrs. Peterson to post her package.

Giving in to his growling stomach, Duncan walked over to the café. The sooner he got a housekeeper, one who could make meals, the better. Then, all this foolish talk would stop. He was a man filled with hunger. That was all.

But it wasn't. He knew that. There was longing, too, alongside that hunger. But it didn't do any good. He didn't know what to do about it, and so it was better not to do anything.

Maggie greeted him as he entered the café and took a seat. A few moments later, a large wedge of apple pie with a slice of cheddar on the side met him.

"Sorry, we only have the apple today," Maggie said apologetically. "Sold out of everything else. Since I've got four apple pies made, got to sell them before Carissa makes anything more."

She hurried away to go help another customer who came in, and Duncan ate his slice slowly, alternating with small bites of the cheese. He hadn't seen Carissa yet. Would she walk out from the kitchen? He wouldn't admit, not to anyone or himself, that he wanted to see her. But, seeing as they were friends, it would be a friendly thing to just say hello.

And the more he reminded himself of that word, *friends*, perhaps the quicker it would sink in.

A few moments later, Carissa walked out into the café to wipe some tables off. When she caught sight of him, she smiled and stepped over closer.

"How are you?" she asked.

"Just fine," Duncan said. He gave her a weak smile, suddenly not really wanting to talk much, even though just moments before he'd been hoping to see her. Alyssa had put him in a foul mood, and while he knew that wasn't Carissa's fault, it was because of her, and he didn't want to say anything that might come off wrong.

"Did you hear about the fundraiser for the children's books?" she asked. "It sounds like a wonderful idea, and sure to raise all that's needed for the children."

"Yes. I did," he answered, his voice tight. He tried to relax, but his legs and shoulders were tense. "Alyssa at the post office told me. I'll be sure to donate some money toward the books."

"Just donate?" Carissa asked, a hint of surprise in her voice. "You aren't planning to bid on a pie?"

The rest of the night, Duncan was sure he would be regretting what happened next, as this was the moment he stuck his foot in his mouth. But it rushed out faster than he could stop it.

"No, I'll donate money. I'm not doing something as foolish as buying a pie," he told her, throwing down his napkin onto the table. The moment the words hit his ears, he cringed at the sound.

"Foolish?" Carissa's eyes were wide.

"That's right. I won't bid on a pie.

When you do, some people expect things you aren't willing to give. You don't know what you're going to end up getting. You don't even know if you'll end up liking it. I'd rather just give money and let somebody else get the pie."

Carissa stammered. "Oh. I see. I was planning to make one. I've never been to a pie auction. Everyone has seemed so excited about it, and telling me about the last time they'd done one, and what fun it was. I'd... planned to make your favorite pie," she said, her voice now filled with hesitation.

"Well, that's great. Someone will sure enjoy it," Duncan said. He stood up and tossed his money on the table. "I've got to head back. You have a good rest of your day," he told her and then left quickly.

He didn't miss the hurt expression on her face, and he wished he could stop and apologize, but he didn't and clambered up into his wagon. The guilt squeezing at him only added to his upset.

Duncan felt angry as he steered the wagon to the general store for his supplies.

He didn't want to settle down. Why did everyone keep hinting at it? Maggie and the ranch hands—even people he thought were his friends like Gabriel, Alyssa, and now Carissa. Everyone was hinting at it.

Why wouldn't they just leave him alone? Couldn't they tell he wasn't interested?

Oh, he knew he didn't have to buy a pie and spend time with her, but it was sort of an unspoken thing. In fact, a pie auction wasn't really just about the pies. He'd been to one once before, a few months after Gem had run off, which was when he decided never again. To him, it felt it was often little more than a courting ritual. Everyone claimed it wasn't, but usually an attractive young woman's pies would sell for quite a bit in order for the person who bought it to invite her to join him for dessert.

Duncan blew out a deep breath. That would put him in a bad position if he was to bid on Carissa's pie or anyone else's. A man didn't want to feel obligated. What part of that didn't anyone understand? If there was one thing that he had learned from Gem, it was that you couldn't take people at face value.

There was always some sort of ulterior motive bubbling up under the surface. Sooner or later, it would come out. Maybe he had just seen a glimpse of Carissa's when she mentioned that she would be making his favorite pie. She didn't say a *pie*. She said his *favorite* pie, which obviously meant she wanted something more than he was willing to give.

Duncan was not going to go down that path. Not yet. He had his plan slow and steady, and while it was true, he hadn't talked to Carissa about it, he assumed she felt the same. And if she didn't, as he was now starting to suspect, well, that was just a sign to him that she was not the right person for him.

No matter what his heart was telling him, this time, Duncan planned to listen to his brain.

Chapter 9

Carissa tried not to let her aunt see her shaking hands as she quickly cleared away Duncan's empty plate and fork and hurried into the kitchen. His words echoed over and over in her mind, seeming to grow louder and louder. Carissa didn't understand. Why had he said that?

She wasn't trying to force Duncan into bidding on her pie. He'd also made it blatantly obvious he was not interested in her as anything more than a friend, so what made him think she'd be hinting to him? She'd only suggested it because she knew how much he liked that pie, and thought that way, he'd have a whole one to himself, and could enjoy it.

There had been no other devious reason. Yes, she did care for him, and did want him to be happy in all things—even something as small as a pie he could enjoy.

But she'd never put her affections in a place they weren't wanted. It would bring her more pain than she had just now.

If that was even possible.

Her chest felt tight and a tear—of anger or hurt, she wasn't sure—forced its way out. Carissa gulped back a sob and wiped the moisture with the back of her hand. Why was she so upset? Was it because he said he wasn't going to the auction? And if so, what about that upset her so much?

Or was it his harsh words? The fact he'd made her feel despicable and conniving and guilty, when she hadn't been wanting to do anything more than make the dessert to participate in the fundraiser, and create a pie she knew he liked.

It didn't matter the reason. He'd left, and with him a piece of her heart. The silence in the café right now was nearly deafening, and the weight of his anger nearly crushed her.

It was different from every other time he'd left.

The thought made her pause. What was it about Duncan that made her feel that strange feeling of loss when he'd left previously? Carissa had never felt such a thing with anyone else. But it was pointless. Just like every other man, he wasn't interested in her in a serious way. Only, this time, he'd come straight out and said it, instead of simply avoiding the topic.

At least before now, she'd been able to pretend at least a little bit that she didn't know how he felt. Even if she had.

No, Duncan had made his feelings abundantly clear.

A tear fell, then another. Carissa hadn't ever let herself feel sorry for the fact no one was interested in her romantically. Until now. The pain was unimaginable. If it had been anyone else other than Duncan, perhaps she wouldn't feel this way. But Duncan...he'd become a friend. Was someone she'd trusted.

And then he hurt her in such an intense way.

"Deepwater is not all I hoped," she whispered, as her eyes swept the town beyond the glass window.

She thought about all the people who had found their way there, like her aunt and uncle. Then there was Laura, seeking a fresh start, Gabriel, the same. Alyssa, looking for similar. Why, even the printer had found love in a woman who had sought refuge here. While it was good they all found it there in Deepwater, she hadn't. Perhaps she needed to leave. After all, there was nothing there for her. Not even a bakery to open.

The kitchen door opened, and Carissa hastily wiped at her face again. It was too late. Her aunt squinted at her. "Are you all right?" she asked.

"Fine," Carissa lied.

"I'm here if you'd like to talk," Maggie said.

"There's nothing to talk about that I haven't already said," Carissa said softly. "No one wants more from me than my ability to make pies or just be a friend."

"That's not true," Maggie said quickly, then she bit her lip. An uncertain look came over her face.

"You see? You know it's true," Carissa said. She wasn't trying to make her aunt feel bad. She wasn't placing blame on her for anything. "It's just how it's always been. There's just something about me, I suppose."

"Here I've done the same," Maggie murmured, sitting down in a kitchen chair. "I wanted you to come to help me at the café because I knew you made wonderful pies. Even though I knew that we were family, and I loved your company, my first thought was about my café. I'm so sorry, Carissa. You didn't deserve my selfishness."

"Oh, Aunt Maggie, that's different," Carissa said, shaking her head as she tried to reassure her. "And truly, I don't mind making pies or doing the one thing I'm good at to help others. I love being here with you. I just want more. And I'm not sure I'm ever going to find it. Especially here."

Maggie nodded, and sighed. "I understand. I do, love. So, you'll leave?"

"There's nothing to keep me here once you are better," Carissa said quietly. "Mama will be happy to have me back, I'm sure. She will continue to put me on display until perhaps someone wants me. With luck, I will want him as well. Perhaps I should give up my lofty idea of not wanting to settle. Perhaps that's been my problem..."

"What about Duncan?" Maggie asked.

Carissa wrapped her arms around herself. "What about him?" she asked.

"I know you care for him," her aunt said gently. "And I know that he cares for you. He's stopping himself from admitting it, and you haven't inherited my pushiness to let him know what you are thinking. Instead, you smile and take every drop of hurt that comes, by pretending you are just fine with nothing more than friendship."

"There's no affection," Carissa said, shaking her head. "You are mistaken. Everyone is. Duncan has made clear—abundantly—just how he feels."

"I know it seems that way," Maggie said, frowning, "but think, just for a moment, if what I said was true."

Oddly, a small smile came over Carissa's face. What if it *was* true? It wasn't, but she could pretend, just for a moment.

"If, and only if, that were at all true," she said slowly, "the problem is, if I won't say anything because I don't want to ruin our friendship, well, not that we have one anymore, and since he flat out refuses to admit it to himself... where does that leave us?" She looked down, her voice low. "I don't want to stay here and feel my heart suffer more than it is. I'll move on. Put this all behind me."

"It feels too much like running," Maggie said, shaking her head. "I'll pray tonight. Pray that you find the path you are meant to have. That an opportunity will open before you, and it will be so obvious, you'll know just what to do."

"Thank you," Carissa said, smiling sadly. "That would be nice. Right now, it's as though I'm standing at a crossroads, and no matter which way I look, it's dark, and storming, and the distance looks menacing."

Neither of them said any more, but sat there in silence, until the café door opened, and they each got back to work, pretending that all was well, even though they knew it wasn't.

That night, when Carissa was in bed and staring at the ceiling, she let her tears fall. She felt so much pain inside of her. Though she'd tried to hope, she'd known it all along. Deepwater held nothing for her. She'd stay until her aunt was able to run things on her own or hire someone to help. For herself, it was time to move away and leave her disappointment behind.

Chapter 10

"You are a fool." Maggie nearly slammed down the plate and fork. His slice of pumpkin pie jiggled with her anger. Maggie's hands were on her hips, and she was glaring at him.

Duncan swallowed hard, not wanting to meet her eyes, but he did it anyway. "I know," he said quietly. "You are right. Everything you've said. I'm in love with Carissa. But I've been fooled once. I'm not letting it happen again."

"And you think my niece would do such a thing?" Maggie scoffed. If it was even possible, she glared harder at him, and Duncan felt like withering under her scorching eyes.

"No," he hastily said, knowing he'd much rather face a rattler in his boot than Maggie's temper ever again.

"You need to get over your past and work on your future." Maggie pointed to the kitchen. "You hurt her feelings, and I can't forgive you for that. That girl has been treated poorly, and I'm ashamed to say I did my share, sending away for her with no thought of anything but how I needed help. Still, she came, and she's done nothing but be kind to everyone, without any sort of ulterior motive. Generous, thoughtful, and caring to a fault is what she is.

"You owe her an apology, assuming she was trying to corner you. Carissa would never do such a thing. She was making that pie because she knows how many people like it. You especially. But even if she was making it for you, because she liked you, if you didn't return those feelings, least you could have done was tell her you'd be there at the auction. You could have let yourself be outbid."

Maggie's face was nearly red, and Duncan felt the same color flash through him. He'd had enough. Guilt and embarrassment and rage—he wasn't sure who any of it was directed at—overwhelmed him. Scraping his chair back, he stood and stalked toward the door, leaving his pie untouched. He didn't say a word, wasn't sure he could or even how he felt at that moment. He just knew he wasn't about to stay there.

As Duncan pushed the door open and forced his way out, he nearly ran right into the reverend. Instantly, his anger dissipated. He wasn't sure why. Maybe it was the way his friend seemed to see right into him. Maybe it was because he was a man of God and it wouldn't be right to be angry around him. It could have even been the calm look on his face and the hand he rested on his shoulder. Duncan wasn't sure.

"Laura baked a cake, and I could use help eating it," Gabriel said with a smile, gesturing back toward the church.

"Sounds good to me. I'm tired of pie," Duncan muttered.

They walked quietly to the church, and Gabriel led him inside and to the small kitchen at the back. A moment later, a thick slice of a pound cake was set before Duncan.

"Thanks," he said quietly.

"Want to tell me why you looked like you were about to explode?" Gabriel asked, setting two mugs of milk on the table.

Duncan shrugged. "Not really."

"That's all right," Gabriel said. "You don't have to. Did it have anything to do with Maggie looking like she was about to come after you to knock some sense into you?"

"I thought you said it was all right when I said I didn't want to tell you." Duncan scowled.

"I did," Gabriel said. "But I sure can't let my friend look so miserable without helping him. And in order to do that, I need to know what the problem is."

"You pry too much," Duncan said, and took a bite of the cake.

"Talk too much too." Gabriel grinned. "At least that's what everyone says." He raised his fork. "But it's my job."

"Annoying people?"

"Helping people," Gabriel corrected.

"This doesn't feel like helping," Duncan grumbled.

"Sure it is," Gabriel said. "You said you were tired of pie. I'm giving you cake. Sometimes a change is good, isn't it?"

"I guess so," Duncan said slowly as his eyes fell to the slice before him.

"And sometimes it's not," Gabriel continued, as if he hadn't heard him.

Duncan looked at him suspiciously.

Gabriel didn't seem to notice. "Sometimes, you just want pie," he went on. "Nothing else will do. Even if you've sworn off it. Said it's not for you. You just want it anyway. You know it with every bit of your being. You think about it at night, think about it during the day, think about it—"

"Are we talking about pie or something else?" Duncan interrupted.

Gabriel cocked his head to the side. "I don't know, are we?"

Duncan wanted to glare at his friend, but how did one get mad at a reverend? Especially one such as Gabriel Sullivan? He was no ordinary reverend.

"I see my friend suffering," Gabriel said gently. "And I remember how my fear, my pride, nearly lost me the one I loved more than anything. I don't want that for you."

"I've been hurt once. I'm not keen for it to happen again." Duncan picked up the mug and looked into it. "I don't think Carissa is the kind of girl to do that, but I'm also too scared to find out. If I...if I don't tell her that I like her, then that won't happen."

Gabriel nodded. "I understand, but without taking a risk, you don't get the reward." He chuckled. "Why, if Laura hadn't have taken the chance on me, things would be very different right now. A piece of my very being would be gone. Only, I'd have never known it, and spent the rest of my days wondering what was missing and how to find it."

"I don't want that. I also feel terrible I hurt her. Everything you say makes sense, but I made a mistake," Duncan said.

"I've made plenty of those," Gabriel said. "Remember who I used to be before I was a reverend?"

Duncan nodded. "That's true. But what if she won't talk to me?"

"Then you'll have to convince her to," Gabriel said with a shrug. "The alternative is a life without pie."

"I don't want that," Duncan said quietly. "I want pie. Not cake. Not cobbler. Pie."

Gabriel hesitated and glanced between the cake before him and Duncan. "Are we talking about pie, or something else?" he asked.

"We're talking about Carissa," Duncan clarified.

His friend relaxed. "I had hoped so," he said. "Now, what will you do?"

"I'm not sure," Duncan said. "I need a plan."

Chapter 11

Carissa watched from a café window as the shop she'd considered turning into a bakery had a small stream of men going to and from, carrying in equipment.

She'd recently met the printer—who stood outside, overseeing the navigation of a large piece of equipment—and he seemed excited to be expanding the size of his shop. Samantha Lundy, who was both beautiful and a trained singer, followed once the doorway was clear, carrying a small box filled with loose papers that fluttered in the breeze.

Her hands squeezing painfully against each other, Carissa turned from the window. Miss Lundy had moved to Deepwater just a few months before Carissa had, escaping scandal, Aunt Maggie said, and here she was, already in a relationship with someone, with plans to be married in the fall. The woman practically radiated joy.

Carissa took a deep breath and tried to squash down the envy in her. Just as every other time, it was always someone other than her who had found their life's path leading to happiness and their true love. She was now thinking that there was no such thing for her now.

The three ranch hands, who she'd learned were from Duncan's ranch, still came in and flirted with her. She'd almost decided to see if it went anywhere, even if they appeared to be betting on something, until she realized they were his men, and if she did get serious with one, she'd have to see Duncan every day for the rest of her life.

Going back into the kitchen, Carissa checked on her pie in the oven. It was almost done. The fresh strawberries from Maggie's garden would taste wonderful, and she planned to whip a pot of sweetened cream to go along with it. This pie wouldn't be set out for the café, it would be part of their dinner tonight, along with the café's menu of fried ham and potatoes or fish in sauce.

Her mouth watered at the thought of the pie as she took one more peek at it. Of all the pies she made, this one was one of her favorites. It was also one she'd not made since moving here, and she wanted to be sure the crust was golden, but not too dark.

The kitchen door opened, and Maggie came in. "You've a letter," she said, setting the envelope down on the worktable as she reached for her apron.

"Is it from Mama or Papa?" Carissa asked.

"No, nor your sisters." Maggie shook her head. "I don't know who."

Carissa wiped her hands on her apron and took up the letter. "Oh!" she said in surprise. "It's one of my friends. She married a man who runs a hotel a short distance from home." Carissa settled before the letter and skimmed it. Suddenly, her stomach started to churn.

"What's wrong?" Maggie asked. "You've gone as pale as a sheet."

"I don't know if something is wrong," Carissa said slowly. "Or if what you prayed for has happened." She sat down at the table. "Juliana says their pastry chef is leaving. She is offering me the position there. It pays well, I'd have a room at the hotel, and a small staff underneath me to help with the baking of desserts for the guests."

"My niece," Maggie said, "pastry chef at a fancy hotel. Has a certain ring to it, doesn't it?"

Carissa let out a small laugh. "I don't know about that. But, I suppose I ought to consider it."

"It's a good offer," Maggie said. "And you'd be near a friend."

"I will write to her and ask for more information," Carissa said. "It's not a yes, though, nor a no. I'm not sure yet. I will be honest with her about that, that I need more time to think on it once I have learned more. Besides, I know that you aren't ready to take back your old duties in full."

"Don't you worry about me," Maggie said. "I'll find someone to help me if this is what you want. Alyssa and Laura both have offered, and I don't mind taking them up on it. You need to think about if you feel this is the right thing for you. The right path."

Carrisa looked at the letter, then slowly folded it and placed it into the envelope. "But how will I know?" she asked. Desperation filled her, and she was sure that it leaked through her words. "Every time I've thought something would get me closer to what felt missing, it didn't."

"You don't know that for sure," Maggie said wisely. "Each of those little stops along the way might be getting you closer to your final destination. Just like a stagecoach does."

"That's true," Carissa admitted. "I hadn't thought of it that way."

"And just like on the stage, you get impatient to arrive, but it gets there when it gets there," Maggie said.

Carissa laughed, "And, it's sometimes an unpleasant, uncomfortable trip."

"Sometimes?" Maggie crossed her arms. "You mean you've gotten to ride the stage without all that?"

Her aunt's expression made Carissa laugh even harder. "Oh, Aunt Maggie, I love you," Carissa said. "If I do leave, I'll miss you terribly."

"I'll do the same," Maggie said. "But if you leave, it's with my blessing, and your pie recipes written down and left behind." Maggie winked.

Carissa giggled at her aunt's teasing, but then she grew serious. "There's one thing, though. I hate to leave with this feeling that Duncan and I are no longer friends. Perhaps I should try again to explain to him I wasn't trying to upset him. He stormed out, and I feel like I didn't get a chance to explain I wasn't trying to force him into anything. I wouldn't."

"I know that, dear," her aunt said. "I told him that as well. Duncan is stubborn, and suffering from past hurts, and a man who takes far too long to make up his mind on most things. That doesn't mean he isn't a good man, but I understand your frustration. And your sorrow."

Carissa felt her shoulders slump. "All you've said is true. It's hard too. I do like him. I'd like to spend more time with him. But he's not ready, I see that. I don't know if he will ever be, and then where will I be? Before, I think I'd have been fine knowing we were friends, but that is gone now."

Maggie sighed. "I shouldn't have scolded him about him jumping to conclusions, but he made me so angry."

"You got upset at him?" Carissa asked. "When?"

"A few days ago," Maggie said. "When you were taking Hank his lunch."

Carissa winced. "How bad was it?"

"Pretty bad," her aunt admitted. "That's why I didn't say anything to you. I expect I ought to apologize myself."

"Maybe he'll stop by," Carissa said. "Then you'll get your chance."

Maggie nodded. "Maybe." Then, she glanced out the window. "Looks like the stage just let out. Get ready for the rush."

Carissa started to put rolls and butter on plates, while Maggie went into the café's main room. As the noise in the café grew, Carissa busily put meals in bowls and on plates, then hurried to slice pies to make it faster to serve everyone.

Though the rush was nice, and it gave her something to think about other than her choice of going back home or becoming a pastry chef, Carissa did wonder now and again what she should do. What if she moved to accept her friend's offer? Would her life just be a continuation of the same? Always seeking, never finding?

Or would this move be the right one? It might be better than her mother trying, and likely failing, to find her a husband. Carissa wasn't sure. The only thing she knew was that she'd miss Duncan, and even if she moved away, she'd never be able to stop thinking about him.

If only she'd never said anything about it being his favorite pie she was making. Things might have stayed the same. Friendly. Not as lonely. Of course, there was also a third possibility. That she and Duncan reconciled. But if they did, could she still stay? Knowing that he wasn't interested in romance right now, and might never be?

Even if they never moved beyond being friends, at least she would have had his friendship, though it might always be tainted. Now she had nothing. Not even a glimmer of hope. That was perhaps the worst thing of all.

Movement outside the window caught her eye, and she saw Duncan standing before the café and staring at it. Almost as if he could sense her, his eyes roamed right to the window where she stood.

She wanted to step back, but that would be foolish. He'd already seen her. Besides, she had no reason to hide. She'd done nothing wrong.

Duncan took a step closer, then another. Carissa wondered if he would come to the café. If he did, what would she say? Apologize, even though she'd not been in the wrong? Likely. That was her way.

Her aunt pushed through the door then, and Carissa turned.

"Packed, that's what it is," her aunt said, looking frazzled. "More tea?"

"The kettles are ready," Carissa said.

Quickly, she fixed several trays with cups of coffee and tea, then carried them out to the room for her aunt. Before long, the stage passengers hurried out as one to resume their journey.

Maggie sighed as the last one scurried out the door, and flopped down behind the long serving counter. "Just want to catch my breath a moment," she said, a hand on her lower back. "Stage days make for good income, but are a bit tiring. Thank goodness I am healing nicely."

Carissa nodded. "Of course. Rest as long as you need. It's calm now. Just the cleanup to do. I can take everything into the kitchen myself and wipe down the tables. We can get the dishes done together in a while."

She stepped to a table and began to set dirty dishes onto her tray. The café door opened. Another customer already? Turning, she forced a smile to her tired face. Then her eyes widened. Duncan stood, staring at her.

"Might we go for a short walk?" he asked her. "There's something I want to tell you."

Chapter 12

Duncan couldn't seem to stop glancing at Carissa as they walked down the street and toward the stream, where a few benches sat on the bank overlooking the slow-moving water that ran over smooth gray stones.

A leaf swirled in the air alongside them, and Duncan watched it for a moment, unsure how to start the conversation. Carissa hadn't spoken, beyond a terse "of course" when he'd asked if they could talk. He wasn't sure what to make of that. It was obvious he wasn't the best at communicating. He'd learned that recently.

He cleared his throat. She didn't even glance at him. He was glad the destination was just ahead. She'd have to look at him when they sat, wouldn't she?

They approached the benches, and Duncan was relieved to see no one else was around. They sat, and Duncan tried to gather his thoughts. The stream before them barely trickled. Just like his words.

Carissa glanced at him, then asked, "What was it you wanted to tell me?"

"That I'm sorry," Duncan said, running a hand over his jaw.

"There's nothing to apologize for," Carissa said, though the tone of her voice didn't match the sweetness of her words. "You made your opinion quite clear, in that buying a pie at a fundraising auction could lead to an outcome you didn't desire—in more ways than one."

Duncan was quiet. He ought to explain better. He just wasn't sure how. What had happened with him and Gem was private. Embarrassing. Uncomfortable to talk about.

A few minutes had passed, with neither of them saying a thing. Carissa stood. "I should go back," she said. "Aunt Maggie needs my help."

"Wait," Duncan said. He grabbed at her arm, then pulled his hand back when she looked at it. "Let me at least try to explain."

She stared at him for a moment, and then nodded. After settling back on the bench, Carissa folded her hands on her lap and stared at the stream. "I'm listening."

"See, I was almost married," Duncan started. He wasn't sure where to go from there. "Wait. Let me start over." He tried to organize his thoughts. Once they felt settled, he nodded to himself.

"Right. About five years ago, before my ranch was so big, I met a woman. Gem. She was the daughter of another rancher, one who was quite wealthy. She and I hit it off. I thought I'd found something special. It seemed she thought so too."

"What happened?" Carissa asked, finally looking at him after he was quiet again for a long time.

"I missed a lot of the signs that she wasn't right for me. Or, as she liked to remind me, I wasn't worthy of her. I didn't have as much money as her father. Couldn't provide as much as she'd grown up with. I ignored all that, not being very experienced with talking to women. So, I just let her talk and I tried harder. I was blinded by first love, and thought everything would work itself out."

"I guess it didn't," Carissa said.

"No," he sighed. "It didn't. The day came we were to get married. I waited at the church. And waited. Waited some more. She didn't ever show up."

"I'm sorry," Carissa said quietly. "That must have been very upsetting."

"What was upsetting was I didn't know why. And I was incredibly embarrassed," Duncan told her. "For a long time, I thought there might be something wrong with me. I realized later, it wasn't me. It wasn't even Gem. It was that we weren't meant to be together."

"And that is why you won't bid on a pie at the auction?" Carissa asked.

"It's because I don't feel ready for another relationship yet. Carissa, I might not ever be. And there are certain expectations that come along when a man—especially an unmarried man—bids on a pie baked by a woman who isn't married."

He wanted to add, especially if she was a beautiful woman, like she was, but he was trying to get out of this mess. Not drag himself in deeper.

"I understand," Carissa told him. She tried to smile, but it looked forced. "I wouldn't want to put you into an uncomfortable position. That wasn't my intention at all. I was glad to have a chance to hear why you'd gotten upset. I really didn't understand why you'd said what you had. Now I do."

"I'm glad you don't hold it against me," Duncan told her.

"I don't," Carissa said. She stood again. "I need to get back to help Aunt Maggie. It's near time for the early dinner rush."

"Wait. There's more I need to tell you," Duncan said, desperation filling him. He'd wanted to tell her that he still wanted to be friends. Perhaps even give it time, let things grow. She was staring at him, and this was his chance to do it, but his tongue froze, and his mind wouldn't work. Why did it always do this to him?

Was it because he sensed it wasn't the right thing to say? He worried that though she said differently, she was still upset. What a foolish thing he was considering, telling her he'd like to take things slow. She might not even want to still be friends, thanks to his mistakes.

A full minute passed as he grappled with his thoughts, and Carissa shook her head. "Are you sure you want to say more? It doesn't seem like you want to talk, and honestly, I've heard enough. You've made yourself clear. Very clear. I...I can't take any more. It hurts too much."

She took a few steps away, then turned to look at him. "Just so you know, if you want the pie, it will be your last chance to get it."

The words shocked Duncan into action. "What do you mean?" he asked as he stood, stumbling forward in his haste.

As soon as she explained herself, he'd tell her how he wanted to go back to how things were. Then, let their relationship to grow, but slowly. He willed himself to say the words this time. He could do it. Fix this.

"I mean, I'm leaving Deepwater. It will be soon. While Aunt Maggie wants me to leave the pie recipes, I don't think she'll be able to bake so many each week, along with the meals she makes. That one is a little more labor intensive, so she'll likely save it for special occasions."

Duncan stared at her, his mind frozen. She was leaving?

"Anyway, I just wanted you to know. If you buy it, no one will say anything since I won't be here. Your reputation will be intact." She gave a small, bitter laugh. "Goodbye, Duncan."

Carissa left, but Duncan felt a ripping feeling inside of his chest as she did. The way she'd said goodbye felt so final. She'd also said she wouldn't be there, and his reputation...wait. Did that mean she wouldn't even be there for the auction?

When was she leaving? Where was she going? Why?

Duncan realized belatedly that he should have asked Carissa these questions. But he hadn't. He also hadn't really explained how hurt he'd been by Gem.

Worse, he hadn't had a chance to tell her what he wanted. To let their friendship naturally grow into more.

His legs were shaky as he made his way back to town. He stopped in front of the café and stared at it. Deepwater wouldn't be the same without Carissa here.

Then, a sudden thought struck him. Even though he wasn't involved with Carissa, in order to spare his heart, she'd broken it anyway, by planning to leave.

And it was all his fault.

Chapter 13

"Now, add the sugar," Carissa said, watching as Maggie poured the sugar into the cream she was whipping.

"You make it look so easy," her aunt muttered. "This is trickier than I thought."

"Keep mixing," Carissa said. "You don't want the sugar to be grainy. It's got to dissolve. Beating it will help break it down so everything is smooth and creamy."

Hank sat at a table watching. "You think it will taste good with blueberries in syrup on the top?" he asked.

"I know so," Carissa assured him. "The pie topper is all ready. We just have to get the filling mixed."

She was trying to teach her aunt how to make the cherry cheese pie, with a variation on toppings. So far, they'd done a blackberry and a raspberry.

"Sure tastes good," her uncle said, sneaking a spoonful of the filling. "But we're going to miss you when you go. Not because of the pies, but because of you."

Carissa fought back a wave of emotion at his words. "I'll miss you too," she said quietly.

"You sure you won't stay? I'll build you your own place," he offered.

Maggie nodded, as she continued to whip the cream. "I won't even ask you to make pies."

Their offers, made only from love, warmed Carissa's heart.

"I'm not even crossing my fingers," Maggie added.

Carissa laughed then. "You are both so sweet, and I appreciate you. But it's not about a bakery or pies. It's about trying to make a fresh start. To go into something, knowing exactly what I'm getting into. A job without expectations or hopes."

"That sounds bleak," Maggie said.

"Perhaps," Carissa agreed. "But, to my mind, that just means whenever something good comes along, it will be a wonderful surprise. I've thought a good deal about it, and it could be that part of the problem is I've been expecting something, looking for it within a particular time frame. When it didn't show up, I got disappointed. With no expectation for anything at all, I can't be unhappy."

"True," her aunt said, panting slightly. She stopped and rubbed at her arm. "I'm exhausted. How you do this endlessly, I'll never know. Youth, I suppose."

"It's done," Carissa said as she peered into the bowl her aunt had been mixing, and scraped the filling into the pie pan. "Just need the canned berries on top."

Maggie nodded, and grimly completed the pie. She smoothed the berries and then said, "That was a lot of work."

"The more you do it, the easier it gets," Carissa said. "Though, admittedly, it is still a lot of work."

"Some of the best things in life are," her uncle said. He pushed up from his chair. "Stage is due. I'm heading over to exchange the horses."

Carissa nodded, and started to slice an apple pie. "I'll get these ready," she said. "I've already got the bread and butter ready."

As she loaded a tray with slices, outside in the street, she spotted Duncan slowly leaving the post office. He looked miserable. Carissa wondered why. Was it something to do with her? She'd told him she wasn't upset, when he said something the day prior. Was he worried about something else, or did their conversation weigh on his mind still?

It was true what she'd said. She wasn't the least bit upset. She was hurt. Hurt he assumed something. Hurt it was true. She did like him. Did want him to buy her pie. Wanted to let their friendship turn into something more.

She understood he'd been wounded by someone, deeply. But that person wasn't her. Not once since she'd known him had she pressured him for anything. So, why did he assume she was?

The man infuriated her, and she felt justified in feeling the way she did. In truth, this was the kind of thing a friendship couldn't survive, not when there was such mistrust from one.

"The stage passengers are here!" Maggie called.

Carissa hurried to the café dining room. Her aunt was walking around, taking orders. Carissa did the same. The next half hour went by quickly, and the stage passengers left as rapidly as they'd come, leaving the café empty, with an abundance of dishes to wash.

"A whirlwind as usual," Carissa said, a yawn escaping her. "Goodness! Today it felt more exhausting than usual. You'd think I'd be more used to this by now."

"Yes, indeed," her aunt exclaimed. "I don't mind, though. I love the rush of people. The café is needed, as well. Now that we are a stage stop, the extra customers have been very good for our town."

Carissa silently agreed. She liked it too, even if it was a lot of work, and it was just another thing to be added to her list of things she'd miss. Movement outside the window caught her eye. She watched as a couple crossed the street arm in arm.

"What's wrong with me?" she asked. Then, she startled. "Ugh. I hadn't realized I'd spoken." She gave a wry laugh. "The couple made me wonder why I'm not the least bit desirable to Duncan. Though I've quite given up, I admit, I'm curious."

"I can answer that," her aunt said. "It's nothing about you, it's these men out this way. Too set in their ways, and too scared to take a chance. The ones willing to wink and smile, well, that's all they're about. You are smart to wait for the right one."

"I'm sure you are right," Carissa sighed. "That's why I'm done with it all. I'm going to focus on myself from here on out. On finding a new dream. Starting with working at the hotel."

"Did you mail your letter yet?" her aunt asked.

"Not yet," Carissa admitted. She wasn't sure how to say every time she'd tried to post the letter to her friend, something had stopped her. She knew it was just fear of the unknown. But it was still difficult. Three times now, she'd gone with it in hand, and returned to the café with it still clutched in her fingers.

"I think I'll mail it the day I leave," Carissa decided. "My friend won't mind my coming unannounced. She said in her most recent letter that she'd hold the spot open until she heard from me."

"Won't be the same without you," Maggie said. "But I'm glad you came for a while."

"I've no regrets," Carissa said. Then, she hesitated. "Well, maybe one."

"What's that?" her aunt asked.

"That I didn't just stop Duncan when he was talking and tell him that I didn't care about what had happened. That I cared about the future. I care about our friendship, and if it's more, then I'd be happy. If it's not, that's fine too. But I'd at least like the chance to find out. I don't know why I didn't. Maybe it's because I'd hoped he'd tell me something along those lines. But he didn't. He just stared at me, so much flickering on his face I couldn't keep up. I wasn't sure what to think or say, honestly. Or if I should say anything at all."

"There's still time to tell him," her aunt suggested.

Carissa shook her head. "I don't think so. That might just complicate things. He's made up his mind. Everything he said made that clear."

"Well, it doesn't solve the problem when you avoid saying something," her aunt replied practically. "Isn't that what got you and Duncan into this mess? He's scared to tell you how he feels, and you are scared to do the same."

"He's worried about more than that," Carissa said with a sigh. "He's scared of people talking."

"I wish you two would work things out," Maggie said. "You like him. He likes you. Both of you beyond friendship."

Carissa looked out the window to the spot Duncan usually hitched his horse. "If that's true," she said quietly, "then he wouldn't have had to say a thing. He'd have planned to bid on my pie."

Chapter 14

Duncan rode through one of his pastures, checking that all his fences were in good condition. As of late, they'd had problems with some of the wood weakening, and the cows knocking it over to get to grass elsewhere. It had become a nuisance, and an expense he hadn't counted on.

Thankfully, he had both the manpower and the financial means to take care of the fences. It was a necessity too. After all, the animals were part of what made his ranch so successful, and it was important to care for them.

"An ounce of prevention is worth a pound of cure," Pete said as he rode next to Duncan. "Goes for everything."

"Uh huh," Duncan said. The older man had been chattering away as they rode, and he hadn't really been paying too much attention. He was too busy beating himself up for how his conversation had gone with Carissa yesterday.

Or, rather, how it hadn't gone.

"Yep," Pete continued. "Taking care of something while it's small keeps it from getting unmanageable."

Duncan shot him a look. Was the man trying to tell him something, like Gabriel and his pie talk?

"I expect this will be the last pasture that needs fixing," the foreman continued. "Then, you'll be in fine shape for a long time."

"I hope you are right," Duncan said, feeling some relief that they had been talking about the fences, and not the mess he'd made with Carissa.

The barn rose in front of them, and Pete assured Duncan, "I'll get a group on the pasture first thing tomorrow. Several of them are wanting to go into town the next day for the pie auction, so I expect they'll work hard and fast so they can."

Duncan nodded. He didn't blame them. A bit of a social activity was always welcomed. At least, by most. He wondered if any of them would be bidding on Carissa's pie. It wasn't like he could stop them, but he didn't really like the idea of it.

What if the man who won asked to share it with her? Mark was a real charmer. So was Kyle, and as handsome as the day was long. Then there was Claude—

"You going to bid on a pie?" Pete asked. Before Duncan could answer, he continued, "I hear Maggie's doing a special pie, and that's what I hope I'll win. Her food always melts in my mouth."

"Well, good luck," Duncan offered, without answering the question. Then, he added, "I'm going to head to the post office. I'll be back shortly."

His foreman waved, and Duncan rode to town. Once there, he didn't let himself look at the café. Carissa's words and expression showing how hurt she was were too fresh in his mind and made him feel sick to his stomach. He hadn't meant to hurt her. He knew what that was like, and wouldn't have ever done that to a friend knowingly. Especially not to the woman he'd hoped for more with.

Had he sent her right into the arms of one of his men with his thoughtlessness?

Ducan dismounted at the post office and hitched his horse. He went to the counter, and Peter greeted him.

"Any mail?" Duncan asked, setting two letters from his ranch hands, and one from him inquiring about a head of cattle, on the counter.

"Yes, you've a few letters for the ranch," Peter said. He reached into a small mail slot. As he handed the mail over, he pulled it back. "Wait, sorry. This one isn't yours."

Duncan glanced down and saw a letter addressed to Carissa.

Peter flipped through the mail and then handed him the rest of the envelopes. "There you are. All yours."

"Thanks," Duncan said. "Ah…" He stopped. He wasn't sure how to ask. Embarrassment washed over him, and he turned to go.

"I'm not supposed to talk about another person's mail," Peter said. "But she's had a few from this same address, if that's what you were wondering."

Duncan didn't answer. If he'd said he wasn't, that would have been a lie. So, he just nodded, and headed to a small bench to sort through his own mail. That it happened to be within view of the café was purely coincidental.

All the letters given to him were for his hands. Beck would be glad to get a letter from his ma. From what Duncan recalled, she'd been going around visiting her sisters in different towns, and Beck worried about her traveling alone.

His eyes drifted through the café windows. He knew he was seeking Carissa, but he didn't care. The café door opened, and the sound of laughter spilled out. Duncan wondered what was going on. Through the window he could see his man Kyle. He was supposed to be back on the ranch.

Did that mean Claude or Mark were there? Or worse—were they not there? Did that mean Carissa had chosen Kyle?

Hesitatingly, he stepped closer. If he was smart, he'd get on his horse and leave. But hadn't he been doing that? Leaving when maybe he should have stayed?

He recalled the letter Carissa had waiting for her, and wondered who it might be from. The only way he'd ever know would be to ask her. And to ask her where she was going. Why she was leaving. All of those questions that he should have asked yesterday.

And then there was all that he should have told her yesterday. About how he did like her. Did want to see where they went, if she was interested in him too. Just...he wanted to go slow.

Duncan tried to ignore his sinking heart as he shoved the letters into his saddlebag. He'd never had many regrets in his life, but this had the potential to be one.

Oddly enough, even his experience with Gem hadn't been a regret. He realized how lucky he was, actually. He'd escaped a lifetime of misery. But this—Carissa—if he left things the way that they were, Duncan knew he'd regret that for the rest of his days. He'd be right where he wanted to avoid. Miserable. Lonely. He also might not have a chance to make amends.

Soon, she'd be gone. He wasn't sure where. Or with whom. The man in the letter, maybe? Had...had someone offered her marriage? Duncan swallowed hard. Was it a man she knew well? Loved? She hadn't talked about anyone, so maybe she'd answered a marriage ad. Had they been trading letters, if the man had written here several times?

Of course, there could be a simple explanation. Females often had male relatives write them. Perhaps it was just that, and he still had a chance.

Then, he remembered the sound of the laughter, and seeing Kyle in the café just now. Had Kyle proposed? Or was he planning to do that once he bid on her pie? Did that mean if they got married, she'd be living in one of the small houses he had for his men?

The thought made him feel sick to his stomach. His hands started to shake, and his head spun.

That meant he'd see her every day. Remember how foolish he'd been. Recall each mistake, and each time he'd shot himself in the foot because he was scared.

He glared off in the distance and curled his hands into fists. Why would she do that, when she could have had him?

But he knew the answer to that.

Because he'd been stupid. Because she didn't have him. He'd never given himself, and she had no idea how he felt.

The idea came to go and tell her. To make her listen this time. But he couldn't. There had been too much hurt in Carissa's eyes. She'd told him she'd had enough, and he didn't blame her. His fear had likely just ruined his chance at the future he wanted. Without a doubt, it had ruined his friendship.

And Duncan wasn't sure which was worse. Right now, they were both about the same, as each meant he couldn't ever have the woman he'd fallen in love with.

Chapter 15

Carissa waved as she left the post office. She'd spent the morning visiting several of the people she'd become friends with over the last few months—namely Laura and Alyssa.

It had been hard to tell them goodbye, and over cups of tea and spice cookies, there had been a few tears, but they'd agreed to write, and promised to stay friends. Carissa knew she'd miss them deeply. She'd never had such good friends before, and she hated knowing that she might never get to see them again.

Regret nagged at Carissa, but what else was there to do? She needed to move forward with her life. Not stay in a place where she felt stuck or unwanted. It felt good, hopeful even, to think about being the pastry chef at her friend's hotel. And, it wasn't but about an hour from home, so she'd be close to her mother and sisters again.

Her father had just written and told her they wished her the best and even planned to stop by for a meal once she was there.

Her mother had, of course, added a note that perhaps she'd even meet a husband there, and they were excited for her future opportunities. Carissa had started to roll her eyes. But then thought, who knew? She didn't, which was why she wasn't going to have any more expectations. Not hers, not those from others. She'd live life curious and open to what it might bring her.

Honestly, the idea of doing that felt very freeing. As though some of the weight had lifted off of her shoulders and some from her heart.

Easing the café's kitchen door open, Carissa walked inside. Her pies for dinner were nearly cooled, and tonight she'd start making her pie for the auction. It had been a terrible thing, the loss of the school books, but it was just astonishing to her how everyone—even those without children—were pulling together to support Gabriel in his fundraising idea. It made her proud knowing that one of her pies would serve a purpose of more than just to feed a body or comfort a soul. It would help get books into the hands of those who most needed and longed for them.

Maggie told her the turnout would be the biggest Carissa had seen yet. The thought made her smile. Deepwater was filled with good people. The town had quite grown on her. She'd miss them more than she imagined when it was time to leave.

An hour passed as Carissa helped her aunt get the meals ready for dinner guests. They sliced pie, set rolls and butter on plates, and got the tables set with forks, spoons, knives, and napkins, all in a bid to make things go smoother once people came in.

Maggie was in the back attending to the final stages of her meal preparation, and Carissa was setting out the last of the napkins when the café door opened. She turned with a smile, ready to greet their first diner of the evening, and tried to keep it from falling when she saw who it was.

Duncan glanced around, almost hesitantly, before he saw her. "Hello," he said. "Okay if I get a bite?"

"Of course," Carissa said, forcing herself not to look away. "That is why the café is here. Full meal or just dessert?"

"Meal," he told her, making his way over to the table by the window he usually took.

She nodded. "Pork and beans or chicken and rice today. Which do you want?"

"The chicken," he told her. He grimaced. "We men make enough beans as it is."

Carissa didn't answer, only gave a polite nod and hurried toward the kitchen. When she went through the door, Maggie looked at her.

"Want me to serve him?" her aunt asked.

"No, it's okay. I will," Carissa said.

"Give him those rolls there," her aunt said, gesturing, "and a piece of your mind."

That made Carissa smile. And laugh. "Maybe I will," she said lightly, though she had no intention of doing so.

A moment later, she set the food in front of Duncan and turned to go.

"Wait," he said. "Please?"

There were no customers yet, so Carissa had no excuse to leave. She nodded, and glanced back at him.

"I want to apologize," he told her. "I also didn't get to say all I'd wanted to say."

"You said enough," Carissa said quietly. Then, before she could help herself, she added, "That's why I never said all *I* wanted to say."

"What do you mean?" Duncan asked.

Carissa thought for a moment, then she said, "It's not important. I know you won't be at the pie auction tomorrow. I'll be leaving soon, though, and I'd rather our last interaction—if that's today—be on a good note."

"Why are you leaving?" Duncan asked. His eyes met hers, and Carissa tried to ignore the flutter that started in her stomach. It was nerves, for her speaking up for herself, she was sure. Though, that didn't make her feel any better about them.

"It's time to," she answered, giving him a tight smile. "That's all."

"People are going to miss you," Duncan said. "Do you really have to go?"

"Are they?" Carissa asked, letting her eyes roam the street. "I'm sure a few will. But most won't notice the lack of anything in this town except for the variety of pies."

"I will," Duncan answered, his voice low. "What are you going to do instead?"

"What I'm best at," Carissa answered. "Go somewhere, make pies, and watch others live out their lives."

"That sounds lonely," he told her. "I should know. Well, except for the making pies part. I don't know how to do that."

"Does it? I suppose it is, a little," Carissa agreed. She leaned against the table next to his, and shrugged. "But here, or there, it doesn't matter. Things will always be the same. It's time to go. I don't have a reason to stay. There's nothing here and no one for me."

She met his eyes on that last part, almost daring him to say something to the contrary. To her disappointment, he looked down at his meal.

"Are...are you sure?" Duncan asked. His eyes flicked toward her own. "What about Maggie? Or...or..."

When the silence had stretched past comfort, Carissa shook her head. "You still can't say it, can you? Even now." She gave a bitter laugh. "You were right. I did like you. I did want to be more than friends one day. But you were also wrong. I wasn't trying to force my feelings on you.

That's why I said nothing. Tried to be content. Until you said what you did, and made it as though my trying to do something—that everyone else in town was doing—was some sort of offensive thing to you."

"I didn't mean—"

"It doesn't matter," Carissa said, her throat tight. "You can't take it back now. It doesn't make a difference, anyway. What happened, did. I'll be gone soon. You don't have to worry about anyone or anything, especially me."

She turned and hurried into the kitchen, ignoring his calls. Maggie held her tightly as Carissa's tears seeped out and turned into silent sobs. Maggie placed a cup of tea in her hands, then left to serve the guests who were trickling into the café in larger numbers.

After a few moments, Carissa rose and began filling plates and bowls numbly. Maggie had said she'd do it all herself, but Carissa wasn't going to do that to her aunt.

After a while, her aunt returned, shaking her head. "He's still out there. Sitting. Hasn't touched his food. I know it's not my cooking. Not a thing wrong with that."

"I don't care," Carissa said, pressing her lips together.

"I do. He's taking up a table," Maggie grumbled. "More than that, he's upsetting my niece. If my back were better, I'd hoist him out myself."

Carissa laughed, though it was a half sob. "You'd do it, too," she said. "I wish I could see it."

"I will say, whatever you told him has set his mind to turning." Maggie glanced out the door. "Oh, he's leaving. Still didn't eat. What a waste. Makes it seem as though I cooked a poor meal." She watched through the door a moment longer, then turned back to Carissa. "I've got this well in hand if you want to go lie down."

"I'm fine," Carissa said. "I need to make my pie for tomorrow."

"I do too," Maggie said. She hesitated, and then asked, "Not to change the subject, but I'm going to try peach on one half, apple on the other. How do you think it will turn out?"

"Wonderfully," Carissa answered with a smile. "Let's get started, right after I do the dishes when the café closes."

Later, Carissa lost herself in the soothing pattern of making the pies, and Maggie's endless chatter. She'd miss these moments, but was just as glad soon she'd be on her way. Duncan hadn't even said anything when she'd confessed her affection. That alone told her she'd made the right decision.

She just wished things could have been different. She really would miss Deepwater. Despite all that had happened with Duncan, she'd grown fond of the place and its people.

Chapter 16

"Risk for reward," Duncan muttered. So far, that hadn't worked out too well. He'd sat at the café for nearly two hours. Carissa hadn't come out of the kitchen.

Maggie had kept giving him looks, but he wasn't quite sure what they meant. He'd never been very good at reading others' expressions. It was even worse when it was a woman, and he couldn't tell if she was just a little upset or downright angry.

By the time he realized his food was still sitting in front of him untouched, it was not only cold, it was getting dark outside.

He'd left, feeling pretty embarrassed he hadn't eaten, and also pretty miserable. His appetite had completely fled, he was so focused on what had just happened. Here, Carissa had admitted what he'd wanted her to. That she had feelings for him. It should have made him feel smug, knowing that he'd been right about her. It didn't, though. And instead of saying something, confessing that he felt the same, like the fool Maggie said he was, he'd just sat there.

Was it shock? Fear? Just flat out hoping he'd have a chance to talk to Carissa again? Duncan wasn't sure. Every emotion possible seemed stuck inside of him right now.

When she'd left the dining room for the kitchen, he'd hoped she'd return. He'd thought about going after her, but he'd seen Maggie chase Hank out once with the large wooden spoon she kept in her apron pocket, and he wasn't anxious to get hit with it.

Then, the café started to get busy. He was sure she'd return. He could catch her then. Only...she hadn't. Maggie had moved at a frantic pace, only stopping once and again to cross her arms and glare at him.

Things would have been simpler, no doubt, if Gem had never come along into his life. She'd ruined his trust and his confidence in relationships. Left him always suspecting the woman would play him false. Filled him with humiliation, and confusion, and fear. He didn't want that again.

A thought startled him, and as he mulled it over, he disliked it. Wasn't that just what he'd done to Carissa? The woman who didn't deserve that at all?

Duncan had never cared for taking risks—before or after Gem. But he knew Gabriel was right. If you took a risk, there was the possibility of the reward.

He rode his horse into the stable, removed the saddle, brushed it down, and then made sure it had water and food. As he walked back to his house, he watched the sun dip lower until only dusky blues and purples showed.

He studied the sky as he turned over his options in his mind. He could leave things as they were. Didn't even have to go to town or tell her goodbye. But he didn't want to tell her goodbye. He wanted to tell her, "Carissa, I like you. I want to see where we could go, if we tried."

It was too late, though, he was sure. She'd be leaving soon. But when? And could he stop her, somehow? He'd had plenty of chances and blown each one.

Duncan thought back to what Carissa had said. How she had liked him. But knew he wasn't looking for more so had kept quiet. Her face held nothing but the truth. Just hearing her say that again made regret and guilt swell up even bigger than it already was in him.

He'd only been thinking about himself, with his plan to take things slow. He also hadn't even consulted her. She had been selfless, thinking about him and what he wanted, before thinking about what she wanted.

She hadn't fallen at all for his hands. She'd been waiting, saving all of her attention for him. A woman like that was special. And he didn't deserve her. It was just as well she hadn't come back out of the kitchen, and they hadn't said goodbye. His heart couldn't handle the burden of knowing he'd made the biggest mistake in the world and lost someone who was better than good for him. She was perfect.

It seemed everyone in town had known how the two of them felt. He'd kept trying to ignore it. Pretend it wasn't so. But his was for a selfish reason, and Carissa...she'd done it out of love, and kindness, and friendship. How long had she liked him? It really didn't matter, but knowing she had but had kept quiet for his sake made him appreciate her even more.

And feel even angrier at himself.

Duncan drew in a deep breath, and went to his study. He sensed the night ahead was going to be long and difficult. Of his own making too. And that's what was making him feel even worse.

What he needed was an idea. A way to make things better. His first plan, talking to Carissa and telling her about Gem, hadn't worked out so well. Maybe this time he needed to tell her how he felt.

Starting with what he should have said much sooner. He thought he might be in love with her, but wanted to take things slow first.

That is, if it wasn't too late.

Chapter 17

"Are you all packed?" Maggie asked, standing in the doorway of Carissa's room above the café.

"Almost," Carissa said, glancing about and reaching for a small stack of books. She placed them in her open trunk, then sat on the bed with a sigh.

"It's not too late to change your mind," Maggie said hopefully. "It's never too late. Why, you could get on that stage and then get right off a minute later and no one would say a thing."

Carissa gave her a sad smile. "Oh, Aunt Maggie, Deepwater was your fresh start, as it's been for so many others, but it's not mine. I've been here several months, and instead of moving forward, I feel stuck. Worse than that, I feel heartsick. Part of that is my own making, and perhaps you think I'm running away, but..."

She stopped for a long moment. But what? In truth, she wasn't sure. Anything she could say would sound like an excuse. Her mother had once told her—wisely—that anything one said that had the word "but" in it was dangerously close to an excuse, if not one already.

"Perhaps I am running away," she finally said. "Just I'm not sure what else to do. All I know is I don't want to experience the heartache of seeing Duncan and knowing we can't be. Worse would be if the right woman came along for him, and I watched them fall in love. It might be cowardly of me, but leaving feels like it would protect my heart, and that's all I want right now."

Her throat tightened, and she whispered, "Can you understand that and not think too terribly of me?"

Maggie nodded, and sat down next to her on the bed. "I'd never think that way of you, my dear, and I do understand. I'm glad you'll be at the town celebration and pie auction, at least," she said.

"Of course, I will be. I have to see who you upset by bringing in the most money for your pie," Carissa teased, a genuine smile on her face. "A half peach and half apple pie is surely something no other woman will bring."

Her aunt nodded proudly. Then she quickly added, "It's all for a good cause. It doesn't matter how much one makes. I am just doing my part."

Carissa's lips twitched, and she tried not to burst into a fit of giggles. "Have you been practicing that?"

"I have," Maggie said, her eyes gleaming. "And when Mrs. Wilson—ahem. Never mind that. It's to raise money for the children. Our tyke is beside himself. Had been reading a story and wants to know how it ends. I'll make sure to replace that book myself, if the reverend doesn't."

Carissa nodded. All of the children had been upset, and Maggie and Hank's son, who had kept himself busy doing extra work to help fundraise, had been no exception.

"A good book is both a joy and a tool for wisdom," Carissa said. "There will be a fine collection once the auction is over and the books bought. Of that, I am sure."

"Are you about ready to go?" Maggie asked.

"Yes. Let me just brush my hair," Carissa said.

"I'll be downstairs waiting," her aunt told her, and left the room.

Carissa took a quick look at herself in the small mirror and made sure her hair was pulled back neatly. Once she was satisfied with her appearance, she left her room and went to the café's kitchen to get her pie.

"I'm ready," Carissa said, glancing around to see where she'd put her pie.

"So am I. Hank went on ahead to help with the tables, and took our ham and green beans for the potluck," Maggie said. "A pack of children came along and picked up our boy, so it's just us."

Carissa nodded, and together, she and Maggie walked to the church, carefully holding their pies to keep them safe in the crowd. All around them, other people were doing the same. Most everyone was laughing or smiling, their hands full of meal fixings or a pie.

Though she'd had very little appetite the last few days from her conflicted emotions, after Carissa handed over her pie to Laura, watching as she placed it with many more, she went to fix a plate of food. Her stomach growled at all there was.

A short time later, her plate filled with fried chicken, biscuits, green beans, corn, and tomato slices, she joined her aunt on a picnic blanket.

In the distance, she could see most of the town's children playing tag, and a group of men clustered around a wagon, which had a broken wheel.

As part of the town's holiday celebration, there would be speeches and lawn games after the pie auction. Carissa didn't intend to join in, but she planned to watch and enjoy seeing the others have fun. It was a shame that this would be her first and only holiday there in Deepwater. She bet the town was breathtaking when decked out at Christmas.

She ate and half listened as Maggie chatted with others close by. A comfortable, relaxed feeling filled her, and Carissa knew this was another moment that she would miss when she left Deepwater. This town had welcomed her quickly and easily as one of their own. She felt such a sense of community here. Something she hadn't ever felt in the town she'd grown up in.

Deepwater was special, there was no doubt in her mind. Her aunt was right. It wasn't too late to stay. But was there even the smallest reason to?

Carissa's eyes roamed the church grounds. They skimmed past couples and families, and those there on their own. She didn't see Duncan anywhere. She wasn't sure why she'd expected him to be there. After all, he'd said he wouldn't be, but she still felt a hollow inside that he hadn't come.

If he came, she could say goodbye. A proper one. With a smile, and a wish for a good future for him. A promise to stop by and say hello if she ever returned to Deepwater. She could have a few more moments with him to keep tucked inside her memory. Even if it might be painful, at least she could leave knowing she'd said a proper farewell.

There was a loud cheer from the men, and Carissa glanced over to see the wagon seemingly repaired. The man who owned it was shaking hands all around.

Laura came over and sat next to her. "What a wonderful turnout," she said, smoothing her skirt around her. "Look at everyone. There are also far more pies than I had expected."

"Those children will get their books, I've no doubt." Maggie nodded.

"I like Peter's idea of a town lending library," Laura said. "I do hope that we will raise enough extra to buy a few dozen more books. The next problem will be where to store the books for the townsfolk."

"Why not use my bookshelves in the café until you get a more permanent building?" Maggie offered. "I've already got about two dozen books. Consider those a donation from me and Hank. We have them there for the café or overnight patrons. He'll build you another few bookshelves. We have space along the walls."

"Sure will," Hank said, coming over with a plate. "Be glad to. Like Maggie said, we have them there for others to enjoy. We can easily add those others. With the café being open so much, and a central location, it will work just fine."

Laura's face lit up. "That would be wonderful. I know I enjoyed reading some of those books while I waited for the stage to be repaired when I first arrived. Perhaps you'll even sell a few more drinks or food items when people come in to browse the collection," she said.

"Could be," Maggie agreed. "I've been thinking of selling small baked goods just for that reason. Muffins and fritters. How many books is Peter hoping for?"

"A great number," Laura said worriedly. "He wants to start with one hundred, and expand. His dream is one day a thousand."

"My word. Wouldn't that be wonderful?" Maggie gasped. "That many books, all in one place, for people to take home and borrow."

"I agree," Laura said. "Gabriel and I will do all we can to make it happen. In town or on the outskirts, to have the opportunity to learn something new or enjoy a story would provide so much education and entertainment to families."

"It's a fine idea," Carissa said. "Something that will be enjoyed by everyone."

"Make sure you come visit again one day, so you can see it," Laura told her warmly. "After all, your pie will have helped create it. I am certain you will have multiple bidders."

Carissa nodded absently. She didn't say more as her aunt and Laura continued to talk. Her eyes resumed roaming around. She wished Duncan were here. It hurt that he wouldn't even say goodbye. But truthfully, what did she expect? She'd gotten upset at him, and left. That was of her own doing. She should have just held her tongue. Did she really think he'd want to see her again after that? He likely didn't even know when she was leaving. He might have thought she had already left.

Her aunt and Laura's conversation drifted around her.

"...if he knew what he wanted," Laura laughed.

Carissa hadn't heard what they were discussing, but she knew what she wanted. And that was to see Duncan again. For things to go back to how they were, neither of them hurt or upset or in pain. But as wonderful as that sounded, the fact remained that was unlikely. This wasn't a book, like on the café's shelf, where there was a happy ending. This was real life, where words and actions had consequences. Very real ones, at that.

Gabriel came over just then, and Laura rose and dusted herself off. "Is it time?" she asked, brushing back a strand of her long dark hair that had come loose.

"Yes," he told her with a grin. "I need your help. I don't trust myself around that many pies."

The women all laughed.

"Then let's go." Laura winked. "I've got a job to do. Maggie, good luck with your pie."

"I don't need luck," Maggie replied, with her own wink. "I happen to know the reverend likes both apple and peach pies. I'm sure to bring top dollar."

Everyone laughed again, and as Laura and Gabriel walked away, Carissa joined her aunt and uncle as they moved closer to where the auction was to be held.

Though she knew it was pointless, her eyes still searched, hoping for just a glimpse of Duncan.

Chapter 18

Duncan watched as his ranch hands rode off toward town. Above the horses' hooves he could hear their excited talking. Beck was sweet on a young woman who was making a cherry pie. He'd brought five dollars in hopes it would be enough.

There was more than a little extra happiness as well, as they would enjoy a meal they hadn't cooked, making Duncan decide he was going to place an ad for a cook for the men first thing tomorrow morning. There was just no reason not to.

Despite the fact he wasn't planning to even attend, Duncan had let himself get caught up in the excitement of his men—at least until that moment he heard Kyle was bidding on Carissa's pie.

Kyle was going around bragging he was determined to get Carissa's pie, and Mark and Claude were betting he wouldn't.

Duncan's hands had balled into fists, and it was all he could do to pretend he hadn't heard. Pete had given him a look when Duncan said he had a few things to do around the ranch and he wasn't joining the rest of the men, but the man hadn't said anything. His headshake and pressed lips spoke louder than any words could.

Now alone but for the animals on the ranch, Duncan went inside the house and found himself pacing from room to room. He tried to work a little at his desk, but frustration at the situation filled him.

Then, he decided. He didn't want to go, but he would. Just to watch. See who bought Carissa's pie. Maybe he'd even bid on it. He sure as anything didn't want Kyle to have it.

But if he did, then that meant that she'd think he was interested in her. There was his problem again.

Because he was interested in her. But she didn't know that. There was also the possibility that she'd accuse him of bidding just to apologize. That might make her feel worse, that it was done out of pity.

Duncan ran his hands through his hair, hating every minute of his indecision. That was another thing Gem hadn't ever liked. How he took too much time to think things through. This was no different.

It was just the price was too high. There was a lot at stake, and a good deal to consider, as he weighed each consequence. What was the right thing to do?

Duncan hesitated, then took to his horse. He rode to town. Not intending to go, but just give his donation. That was allowed. He would just hope that Kyle didn't win Carissa's pie, or that if he did, she didn't eat with him. If she hadn't left town yet.

He wasn't far from the church when he saw Postmaster Peter, who waved at him.

"Hello!" Peter said. "Going to bid? I'm after a pie to surprise the Larson family with. They've got a baby coming any minute, so aren't making it today. I thought that might be a nice surprise."

"It will be," Duncan said. "That's mighty nice of you."

Peter shrugged. "I know a lot of people think a pie auction is some sort of thing to spend time with a sweetheart, but not for everyone. Especially those of us with a sweetheart. We just want the pie! Alyssa wants to bid herself if a blackberry comes up."

"I wish you both good luck," Duncan said. "I was just going to drop off my donation."

"You really not going to bid on anything?" Peter asked curiously.

Duncan shook his head. As if his horse could feel his unease, the mare shook her head as well and huffed.

Peter gave him a considering look, then said, "It's never too late to change your mind."

The church appeared before them, and a large crowd was gathered on the lawn. Peter hurried over to Alyssa, and Duncan settled himself in the shadow of a large tree. He was close enough to see and hear everything, but hoped he was far enough back no one would notice him.

It was starting. Gabriel was holding up a pie, and talking about it. "Sweet potato pie! A delight for the tastebuds, and a help for the students. Made by…"

Duncan let his eyes wander as he searched the crowd. Was Carissa here? He spotted Hank, and a short distance away was his boy playing with some of the others. But he didn't see Carissa.

The pie sold, and another, a honey pie by Mrs. Wilson, started with heavy bidding. Duncan scanned the crowd again. Then, he saw her. Carissa stood near her aunt. They were watching intently, but also laughing at something Maggie had just said. He held his breath when he saw her. She was beautiful. Not just her appearance, but all of her.

Her pale pink dress brought out hints of red in her hair. She was somehow always so neat, even though she worked all day in a kitchen. Duncan marveled at that. No one was perfect, he knew that, but Carissa came just about as close as one could get. In her short time here, she'd always given of herself and her time freely. Something many never did.

He regretted how he'd made her feel. How he'd hurt her. Duncan pressed himself closer to the tree. He didn't want to be seen. Didn't want Maggie to start in on him, or accidently say something that would make Carissa feel hurt again. But he wanted to apologize to her. Right after the auction, he would. He'd never have another chance, and wouldn't waste this one. At least they could part as friends. It wouldn't be what he wanted, but it would be a start.

The honey pie sold, then a pumpkin. An apple pie sold, then Maggie's half apple and half peach came up for bid. Duncan crept closer, watching in surprise as the price went higher and higher.

He thought about what Peter had said. About how some people just wanted pie. He did too. But he didn't just want pie. He wanted Carissa.

Duncan swallowed hard as Gabriel reached for another pie. He knew just whose it was.

The reverend held it, and called, "A cherry cheese pie. You know how good it is. Made by Carissa. Let's start the bidding."

Duncan's head turned side to side as bids started, flying faster than he'd ever thought possible. Carissa looked stunned as well, as the number went higher and higher. Maggie let out a squeal, and grabbed Carissa's arm in her excitement.

Higher and higher it went, and Duncan searched the crowd. His heart sank when he caught sight of the bidders. Duncan turned to walk away. There was no point in watching. His heart couldn't stand it.

Chapter 19

Carissa squeezed her aunt's hand as Maggie's pie ended up going for twenty-one dollars. Maggie looked thrilled, but when someone Carissa wasn't familiar with congratulated her, her aunt shook her head humbly, and said, "It's for the children. I'm just happy it fetched such a high price to help them."

It was hard not to smile at her aunt's comment, but when Carissa saw her pie next, the laughter that had been bubbling up inside of her fled, replaced entirely with shock.

"A dollar!" a man shouted.

Her head twisted to see who had called it out, when Kyle, Duncan's ranch hand, stepped forward. "Three dollars!"

Another voice, and another person she couldn't see called out, "Four!"

"My goodness," Maggie whispered. "I bet yours fetches as much as mine does! Maybe even more. Listen to them."

Carissa didn't answer. She was too busy glancing around. She couldn't see who the last bidder was. A worry filled her then, reminding her of something Duncan said.

"Aunt Maggie," she asked, panic filling her, "what if I don't want to share the pie with the winner?"

"Then you won't," her aunt promised. "I'll stay right by your side and chase him off if I have to." She reached into her pocket. "Just so happen to have my wooden spoon with me."

Any other time Carissa might have laughed, but today, relief filled her, and she nodded and stood tensely, waiting as the numbers grew higher.

"Six dollars!"

"Seven!" Kyle called.

"Ten!" the voice from behind her somewhere said.

Gabriel was pointing to different men, but Carissa still couldn't see who the third bidder was. The first dropped out, shaking his head as he walked away, but Kyle stood firm, his jaw clenched.

A shiver of fear went through her. While it wouldn't be horrible to sit with Kyle after the pie auction, Carissa had the feeling that he was bidding for more than just her pie.

That he was bidding because he wanted her or wanted to win some bet.

Kyle whispered to someone next to him, who nodded and reached into his pocket. Carissa saw a handful of money dropped into his palm, and Kyle called out, "Twelve."

Her stomach felt sick as Gabriel pointed to the person she couldn't see. "I have a bid for fifteen," he called.

Carissa couldn't help but feel a flutter of worry go through her. She wished Duncan were here. If only he'd come. Even if he didn't bid. Then, she'd have a reason not to spend time with whoever bought her pie. Yes, her aunt had her spoon, and Carissa didn't doubt she'd use it, but Carissa wasn't sure she could let her aunt risk her café business because of her.

Once more, she scanned the crowd. It was so thick, though, she couldn't see beyond a few people.

"Twenty!" the unseen person said.

"Twenty-two," Kyle shouted.

Carissa's lips trembled. Her head felt light, and her hands were shaking. The suspense was becoming too much. She couldn't wait to leave. A fresh start waited for her. Despite what Duncan had said, she'd hoped he'd still show up. But he wasn't there. It was obvious he didn't care. If he had, he'd have shown up.

"Thirty!"

She inhaled sharply. Thirty dollars? For a pie?

Who was the man bidding? Her thoughts were torn between wondering, and the fact she was angry. She told Duncan she'd be leaving after the pie auction. He couldn't even show up to tell her goodbye?

"Thirty-four!" Kyle called. He looked worried.

Gabriel glanced somewhere behind her. "We have a bid for thirty-four," he said. "Anyone want to go higher?"

Her chest was tight. Carissa's mouth was dry, and she felt like she couldn't breathe. Her eyes were locked onto Gabriel as he nodded to the person she couldn't see. His eyebrows shot up, and he asked, "Are you sure?"

There must have been a confirmation, for the reverend looked over at Kyle. "We have a bid of one hundred dollars. Will you go any higher?"

There was a collective gasp. Carissa's head felt light, and her stomach queasy. Who had that much money to spend on a pie? Surely, at that price, he'd expect her to sit with him.

Once more, Carissa tried to see who was bidding, but she couldn't. She stood on her toes, hoping to see, but too many people had crowded around her.

She glanced at Kyle. He had a scowl on his face, which then turned into a good-natured expression when he saw who the bidder was. Carissa felt irritated. She wanted to see too, but she didn't know where they were, and wasn't tall enough to see over the people clustered around.

The crowd behind her was moving, as Gabriel called, "Clear a path! Let the winner through!"

Steeling herself, Carissa turned to see who it was. Her stomach felt queasy as she searched each face to see who was stepping forward.

Chapter 20

Duncan made a stop motion to Kyle, but his ranch hand just smirked, and bid again. Duncan was surprised he didn't catch fire, as he was sure smoke was coming out of his ears.

The bidding grew more intense. He glared at Kyle, who was now pointedly ignoring him. The two of them would be having words later. Especially if the man won Carissa's pie.

Duncan could see Carissa looking around, trying to see who kept outbidding Kyle. There was a worried look on her face. Was that because she didn't want Kyle outbid? Or because she couldn't see who was bidding against him? Duncan's hands clenched. He hoped it was the latter. If he knew Carissa as well as he hoped, he thought she'd be nervous at the idea of ending up with someone she wasn't comfortable with asking her to join him after the auction.

"Thirty-four!" Kyle called.

Duncan had about had enough. What was Kyle thinking? And how did he have so much money to spend on a pie? Gabriel was scanning the crowd. He met Duncan's eyes. Duncan nodded slightly as he held up his fingers.

The reverend's eyebrows shot up, and he asked, "Are you sure?" Then he looked over at Kyle. "We have a bid of one hundred dollars. Will you go any higher?"

The crowd started buzzing with excitement. Duncan watched as the crowd shuffled around, and Carissa vanished from his sight for a moment. When she came back into view, she was scanning the crowd, an expression of near panic on her face.

Duncan caught Kyle's eye. His hand had a scowl on his face, but then he winked, and laughed.

Gabriel called, "Clear a path! Let the winner through!"

Everyone turned this way and that, looking to see who'd placed the hundred-dollar bid on Carissa's pie. That would buy a lot of schoolbooks.

The crowd had stilled now, and a large opening cleared before Carissa. She still looked worried, her eyes frantically scanning for any sign of who it was who had won.

Duncan stepped forward. It was so quiet now, he could hear the leaves rustling in the very slight breeze. His eyes met Carissa's, and her expression changed from worry to surprise. He walked toward her, then stopped, about two steps away.

"I'm sorry," Duncan told her. "I was a fool. I was scared. I was a whole lot of other things too."

He waited, making sure she heard him before he continued. He didn't even care that everyone in town was there, listening, watching. Whispering. Maggie had her handkerchief out and dabbed at her eyes.

"I like you, Carissa. I think I probably love you, something I never thought would ever happen again. I've made a lot of mistakes as of late, the first being that I didn't tell you I don't want you to leave. That I want you to stay. With me."

Duncan moved closer to Carissa. She was nearly frozen, staring at him with wide eyes.

He cleared his throat, and continued, "I want to court you, and love you, and be with you. If you'll let me."

She still hadn't answered, and Duncan wasn't sure what to think. He was growing nervous and hoped he wasn't starting to sweat. What if he passed out? Did men do that? He knew some women did. Duncan tugged at his collar. It felt like it was shrinking.

Someone in the crowd called out, "Answer him!" and it seemed to break the spell that had come over her.

Carissa smiled and threw herself into his arms. Everyone laughed and cheered as Duncan spun her around, and then called out joyously, "I'm here to claim my pie!"

Gabriel appeared, holding it. "I'm happy to trade it," he grinned, "in exchange for your most generous donation."

"I can't believe you came," Carissa whispered, as it seemed to finally strike her that he was there, and had been the mysterious bidder of her pie. "And I can't believe you spent one hundred dollars on it."

"Well worth every penny," Duncan said, as he handed Laura the money.

"Next up!" Gabriel called. "A blackberry pie!"

Alyssa called out, "Three dollars!"

Duncan led Carissa away a short distance. "I am so glad you are here. I had to come. I couldn't wait another moment. As it was, I already knew I might be too late. As for the price...well, I knew I had to do something or else Kyle might have won it, and taken away my chance to talk to you. I'm really sorry, Carissa. I never meant to hurt you."

"I understand," she told him. "All of this might have gone so differently, if we'd just talked things out sooner."

"That's true," he said slowly, "but then, you wouldn't have had a man confess his love for you before the whole town. Or spend that much on your pie. No one will ever top that."

Carissa laughed. He loved how happy she looked. Her eyes had tiny crinkles in the corners that he wanted to kiss. "You are right," she agreed. "Aunt Maggie will have a wonderful time adding this to her collection of stories."

"So it's a yes?" he asked, almost scared to hear her answer. "You never said."

"Oh yes. It's always a yes, when it comes to you, Duncan," Carissa said. "I've waited for you for a very long time. I don't think I'll let you go."

"Sold!" Gabriel shouted. "The blackberry pie goes to Alyssa for seven dollars!"

Duncan grinned as he glanced over and saw the postmaster's wife nearly skip up to accept her pie.

"I like it here," Carissa told him, wrapping her arm through his and resting her head on his shoulder. "I also like you. A lot."

"I'm glad," Duncan told her. He cleared his throat. "I had a plan," he told her slowly. "For us. You know, moving forward? That is, if you wanted to hear it."

"What is it?" Carissa asked.

"We were going to be friends first. Then see about more." He hesitated. "If that worked for you."

"That sounds just fine," Carissa told him. "I'm in no rush. I don't plan to leave Deepwater."

Duncan smiled at her. "I'm glad you aren't leaving. I love you, Carissa."

"Which do you love better?" she asked teasingly, as she walked them toward her aunt, who was staring at her hopefully. "Me, or my pies?"

"You," Duncan told her. "A thousand times you."

Maggie rushed up, and then looked at him. "You made the right choice," she told him firmly. "I'd brought my spoon, just in case."

"You won't need that," Carissa laughed. Then, she leaned close and whispered, "But I'll take one as a gift one day."

Duncan glanced over as Hank clapped him on the shoulder. "Took you two long enough," he said. "But I'm glad this story has a happy ending."

"The best," Carissa agreed. "I'll write my friend and tell her I'm not coming."

"Do you think you'll ever regret that?" Duncan asked, looking at her, concerned. "I don't want you to give up your dream."

"I'm not," Carissa assured him. "I found my dream right here in Deepwater. It was you."

Epilogue

Carissa wrapped her apron strings about her and pushed up her sleeves. Over the past year, Carissa and Duncan had let their friendship grow naturally into something more.

It had given Duncan the time he needed to feel confident she was who she presented herself as, and Carissa hadn't minded at all, as she got to enjoy the courting experience like her sisters had. Perhaps even better, as Duncan was already a friend and each moment with him was simply better than the last.

Duncan had recently hired a housekeeper, who also cooked for the men. He still stopped by the diner often, but Carissa had told him she was relieved he had help, as it would have been too much for her, on top of her baking.

Now, both knowing they were making the right choice, wedding bells were on the horizon.

Before long, her parents and sisters would be arriving to watch her stand before the members of the town as Gabriel pronounced them husband and wife.

"Goodness, it's busy out there," Maggie said, rushing in the kitchen then back out again, a tray of raspberry and sugar cream pie slices in her hands.

With no open storefront, and not really wanting to try and run a bakery on her own, Carissa and Maggie decided to turn part of the café into a bakery. Hank and Duncan were hard at work building a large display case, and had sent away for a large glass pane to help display the baked goods that would be put inside. There would be a selection of small items, perfect for someone to enjoy while reading one of the books on the shelves of the town's one hundred and ninety-seven book collection.

Maggie rushed back in. "Tea? Coffee?" she asked, pushing back the hair that had frizzed its way from her bun.

"It's ready," Carissa said, and hefted the tray. "We need to hire a little help."

"I agree," her aunt said, holding the door for her.

Carissa bustled about the room, serving the stagecoach passengers. A few moments later, they all left in a rush as a bell rang, warning the stage was about to leave.

"Phew," her aunt said, shaking her head at the mess in the café.

"We'll get it," Carissa said. "We always do." As she started cleaning the tables near the window, Duncan walked past and stopped, grinning at her.

"I love you," he said through the window.

"I love you," she answered.

He waved and continued on his way. When Carissa turned, she saw her aunt smiling.

"What are you thinking about?" Carissa asked.

"Just how there's never been a person who's come to Deepwater and not found their happy ending," her aunt said.

"That's because Deepwater is a special place," Carissa said, taking the tray of dirty dishes to the back.

It was true. It was a town filled with special people, and dreams that came true. And Carissa had the feeling that would never change.

The True Story of the Cherry Cheese Pie

In the mood for a sweet, fruity treat, or have unexpected company dropping by? Maybe it's HOT and you just don't want to heat up the oven but need dessert. I've got the perfect and most versatile thing for you.

Before I got married, one evening my mother-in-law served what she called a "Courting Pie." It was a pie served to her and her husband at a get-together that brought them together, and is a piece of their family history.

I'd never had anything like it, and loved it so much! But, as we have some food allergies in our house, I've modified one ingredient of the original recipe so that we can all enjoy it. You'll see the original still listed there, as it's either / or.

Either way you make this, it's incredibly tasty, and all of this is pretty much fridge and pantry staples, so you can whip this thing up in less than ten minutes. You will want to chill it for at least two hours, though.

Cherry Cream Cheese Pie
Ingredients

- 1 block of softened cream cheese

- ½ cup of sugar

- 1 can of pie filling (Blueberry, cherry, or raspberry work best)

- 1 ½ cups of heavy cream whipped into peaks **OR** 1 tub of whipped topping.

- (If using whipping cream, also add 1 tsp of vanilla and 2 tbsp of powdered sugar while whipping into peaks.)

- 1 graham cracker pie crust, made yourself or store-bought

Steps:

1. Beat whipping cream, powdered sugar, and vanilla until peaks form. If using whipped topping, you can omit this step.

2. In a separate bowl, beat cream cheese and sugar until smooth

3. Combine whipped cream and cream cheese mixture. Beat until smooth

4. Pour into pie pan

5. Add pie filling on top

6. Refrigerate for at least 2 hours

Notes:

A can of the pie filling can actually generously top two 8 or 9-inch pies, so consider doubling this recipe! I always do!

Want to try something other than cherry? Blueberry or raspberry pie fillings work wonderfully too.

Don't want crust or don't have pie pans? No need for them! Just put the mixture in a small bowl and top with the fruity topping. It's still amazing. Or, put a graham cracker or cookie in the bottom of a small bowl.

Need to serve a crowd? Make in a 9x13-inch pan and cut into squares.

Visit everyone in Deepwater

Trapped in Deepwater

Together, they are going to have to save themselves...and the town.

Laura Ashborne is convinced she's a walking bad luck charm. Trying to make a fresh start, she sets out on a stagecoach to become a schoolteacher. However, the coach she's on breaks down in the middle of nowhere a few days before Christmas, and she's forced to spend an entire week in the tiny town of Deepwater.

Reverend Gabriel Sullivan wants to help the beautiful stranded traveler, and he'd determined to show her she's not bad luck. But when his dark past catches up to him, he's put into a dangerous situation, and Laura right along with him.

https://www.amazon.com/Trapped-Deepwater-Christmas-Bride-Dilemma-ebook/dp/B0C74R6NW6

***

Alyssa's Desperate Plan
"Yer too small on the top. I want a bigger woman."

Alyssa Moore never expected *that* to be the reason her prospective groom turned her away after one look. Now, with almost no money and no family to turn to for help, she's stuck waiting in a small town until the mail-order bride agency that sent her finds another match. She's embarrassed to seek help because that isn't her only mortifying situation, but it's all she can do.

When an upset woman finds him to ask for help posting a letter, Peter West is more than curious about her. As he learns more, he wonders...what would happen if her letter didn't post? At least for a few days. Would she consider staying there, with someone like him? He knows it's pointless. A beautiful woman like that wouldn't want a man like him.

As Alyssa becomes desperate and Peter tries to summon his courage, they'll each discover there's far more to a person than meets the eye—and that friendship and love can blossom in the most unexpected of ways.

https://www.amazon.com/Alyssas-Desperate-Rejected -Mail-Order-Brides-ebook/dp/B0CN8FKZX7

***

Away in Deepwater

She had the perfect life, until it wasn't . He's hiding to forget. Heartbreak can't heal twice—can it?

Trying to escape a scandal, Samantha Lundy, a talented singer with the voice of an angel, moves to Deepwater. It is her hope this tiny town in the middle of nowhere will both heal and hide her. Determined never to love or sing again so she can forget her past, she plans to become a recluse.

Dirk Schmit is surprised when a package is delivered to his print shop. Upon opening it, he sees it is actually intended for the woman who just moved next door. Curious to meet her, he brings her the package and is stunned to find the very thing he doesn't believe in happens, does. Love at first sight. But Dirk refuses to be more than friendly—heartbreak can't heal twice.

Samantha wants nothing to do with Dirk or anyone else, but as the inhabitants of Deepwater are determined to make her feel welcome, her icy interior thaws. When an opportunity to use her talents to help arise, Samantha wonders if perhaps she can find her voice again.

***

Mail-Order Tailor (Spring 2025)

Josiah Adams seeks refuge in the quiet town of Deepwater, answering the letter for a mail-order husband. He yearns for a mother for his young daughter, Madeline, but the fears from his first failed marriage keep his heart guarded. For his daughter's sake, he'll try again, but when he arrives, the woman who sent the letter is nowhere to be found.

Ginny Waters, the eldest of eleven, possesses a natural nurturing spirit and agrees to take on the role of nanny until the mysterious letter sender, and Madeline's new mother, can be found. Meanwhile, her heart warms to both the little girl and her reserved father.

As the trio fall into a comfortable routine, Josiah finds himself softening toward Ginny. Could there be room for love in his heart again? But what about the woman he was supposed to have a marriage of convenience with?

Suddenly, Madeline and Ginny vanish without a trace, the sender of the mail-order husband letter is made known, and Josiah's world crumbles. Fear and desperate

ion grip him as he searches for answers. Will he ever see his daughter and his new love again?

Note from Author

Thank you for taking the time to read Cherry Cheese Pie by Carissa!

Could I ask for one small favor? Reviews like yours on Amazon mean so much to me and help others to find my books! Even just a single line means a lot!

Also...

Want a FREE book?

Stop by my website to get your no strings attached **FREE book**. It's my gift to you, as a thank you for reading this one.

www.sarahlambbooks.com

About the Author

Sarah writes captivating characters and clean romance that's anything BUT boring! From heartbreaking moments to heartwarming tales, get swept away in either historical or small town romance that pulls you in until the last page.

Nestled in the Blue Ridge Mountains of Virginia where she's married to her Texan husband, you'll find Sarah creating her next book, homeschooling her two boys, or volunteering in her community.

There are other great books in this series as well!

Find all the Old Timey Holiday Kitchenbooks on Amazon!

Want more of Sarah's books? She writes for children and adults! Find them all on Amazon!